THE DSA SEASON ONE, BOOK THREE

THE BRIDGE

Also by Lou Paduano

The Greystone Saga

Signs of Portents
Tales from Portents
The Medusa Coin
Pathways in the Dark
A Circle of Shadows

Greystone-in-Training

Hammer and Anvil

The DSA

Season One
The Clearing
Promethean

THE DSA SEASON ONE, BOOK THREE

THE BRIDGE

Lou Paduano

Eleven Ten Publishing LLC

GRAND ISLAND, NEW YORK

Eleven Ten Publishing LLC
282 Fareway Lane
Grand Island, NY 14072

Printed in the United States of America
Edited by JD Book Services.
Cover art design by MiblArt

First edition published 2019

Library of Congress Cataloguing in Publication Data
Paduano, Lou
The Bridge / Lou Paduano

LCCN: 2019918028
ISBN-13: 978-1-944965-22-8 (paperback)
ISBN-13: 978-1-944965-21-1 (eBook)

For my uncle, Garnet D. Hanson,
and my cousin, Garnet D. Hanson II.
They served with honor.

CHAPTER ONE
Pittsburgh – 1994

She took him to the bridge. Not directly—she knew better than to label the visit in that manner. Instead, their outing was built around another real-world lesson. One day per month the pair ran errands together: they bought groceries under a tight budget, figured out the correct bus route through the city to get to their destination, or helped at the local soup kitchen. These were lessons unable to be gleaned from a textbook or on the playground, though they carried the same, if not more, importance.

The bridge, however, stood apart from such lessons. Gephyrophobia it was called—he'd looked up the affliction at the library one day. A fear of bridges. His wasn't a natural one. No, his came from his older brother, Dante.

A year earlier, the pair had traveled along the Panther Hollow Bridge near their home in Pittsburgh. The nighttime jaunt had limited the foot traffic on the bridge running through Schenley Park. Dante, always tormenting the younger man to prop himself up, had decided to take things to the next level. He had pushed his brother, not realizing the precarious footing of his companion. Dante's sibling had fallen, his hand grappling for the ledge as the water rushed beneath him and waited to swallow him whole.

Dante had pulled his brother to safety, and promises were made to never speak of the misadventure—though it wasn't difficult to glean upon their return home. From that moment on, he'd refused to travel via the pedestrian bridge. He closed his eyes tight and held his breath when they approached any such structure in the city. His heart pounded, and his breath turned ragged every time.

Fear won out.

His mother, however, pushed him. The pair stood beside the Smithfield Street Bridge, which stretched out over the Monongahela River. It was a cold day, and a slight drizzle in the air pitter-pattered against their shared umbrella. She held his hand, keeping him close—both to her and to his growing terror.

He chalked his terror up to a loss of control or a fear of hovering over nothing. They were all excuses, and none of them appeased the strong-willed widow. She shuffled him closer, the waves pounding the shoreline beneath their position.

"Bridges carry us," she said in the rain. Her words were clear against the gray sky—strong just like her. "They span the past to the future. Our past carries us ahead, gives us momentum, but it is our drive—our very will—that pushes us to the other side. To the future."

Others had recommended therapy, counseling to overcome his struggle. Some had suggested drugs as a course correction. Neither was a viable option to the mother of two.

"That may work for other folk," she always said. "*We* have to be stronger. Your father knew it. He served his country with dignity. Stood up like a man. Just like you will."

"I can't," the young man replied.

"Can't is not a word we know," she answered. "Not in our house and not out in the world."

"Momma—"

"You look at me," she said, kneeling before her youngest. "You look me in the eye and tell me you can't. You tell me I'm wrong. That you don't have what I see in you. You are strong enough, even now. You let fear take over; and it ain't never giving up its grip. You understand?"

Strength rested in her eyes. Her husband had been killed in combat. His body had never made the journey home. He'd left her with two boys and a lifetime of grief, but the strength remained. She always stood by her children, striving for them to be better to achieve their dreams.

Wrinkles spread from tired eyes, the years beaten into her. She remained a pillar for the boy—a force of nature, always defending her own, all the while willing to sacrifice for others.

"Yes," the child said.

"Good." The umbrella shielded her from the morning shower. She held out her hand. "You coming or not?"

"In a minute?" He stared out over the bridge, the road extending for miles.

"Good boy," his mother said, a hand on his shoulder. "You're going to change the world someday, Lincoln MacKenzie. Believe that."

It was the last thing she ever said to him. He didn't know how long he had stared at the Smithfield Street Bridge, wondering what future might be on the other side for him. He didn't know if it was the sound of gunfire that startled him from the innocent fears of an eight-year-old.

Maybe it was his mother's cry when she fell. Or it might have come later, when the police arrived to tell him how his mother had stood up to a drugged-out kid in a ski mask. How she'd spoken to the boy calmly and rationally in the hopes of preventing the bloodshed that took her life. How, through it all, she remained every bit the strong woman he had known all his short life — sacrificing herself to save the other shoppers.

Lincoln couldn't remember how long he stared that day in the rain. He could never clearly recall the events that had taken his mother from him. All that remained was the bridge and the future ahead.

The terrible, unknowable future.

CHAPTER TWO

Three days.

Lincoln's deadline was clear. The overnight drive had been long from Kentucky to Iowa, but he had remained focused on the task ahead. Questions kept him awake: those pertaining to the mission at hand as well as how much information eluded him. How far ahead his target was worried him and he needed to make up for it before the day arrived.

Des Moines had never interested Lincoln. It was a single stop in what should have become a nationwide tour. Instead, it stood as the symbol of his failure. From the tallest peak at 801 Grand to the Iowa State Fairgrounds in the east, Des Moines had haunted Lincoln's dreams for the last four years.

The Savery sat at the center of his nightmares, and it was there the weary agent arrived early the second day. He rested in his Jeep along the top level of a parking garage attached to the hotel. Four hours of sleep perked him up, and a protein bar and a bottle of water helped him refuel.

Preparation was key and Lincoln was no stranger to it. Location, security, entrances and exits — every piece was critical when planning. Staging operations during his multiple tours in the military had made him a large proponent of knowing the territory before committing to an attack.

He only had one day to make it happen.

Perimeter checks came first. Lincoln circled the area in sweeping arcs. He started three blocks out in every direction, then worked his way to two, followed by one. He timed traffic signals, memorized bus schedules, and scanned the crowds for any sign of his target on the move.

Each aspect added to his confidence. The Witness might have prepared for his arrival, having set the date and place, but Lincoln controlled the exact time for their meeting.

Unwilling to play a shadow game with his target, Lincoln took the offensive. Once the perimeter was secured he switched to the hotel itself. He checked into a room on a lower floor using fake credentials offered from his fully stocked go-bag.

After check-in he started his hunt by surveilling the lobby. He took up position in a corner with clear sight lines in all directions. He monitored all foot traffic through the area, keeping a lookout for the man at the heart of his endeavor while pretending to flip through a magazine.

He also looked for other parties involved. He had been warned of the ticking clock; he knew that after Bellbrook there would be more than a few interested groups searching for the man behind the loss of seven thousand lives. Yet after two hours of waiting in the lobby there was no sign of anyone out of the ordinary.

So Lincoln relegated himself to the rest of the hotel. He tracked security throughout the first floor, noting their movements and their base of operations behind the front desk. To flush out potential problem areas, he identified the security cameras on every floor as well as the server rooms. He sabotaged one camera on the fourth floor without being seen, and he stuck around to see the alertness of the staff. They identified the problem within three minutes: a small window, but a window nonetheless.

The day escaped him, but that was about the only thing that did. Methodical in his approach, Lincoln studied the ins and outs of the Savery until the sun finally settled for the night. Holiday traffic was light, as was his dinner: some chips and the last of his cold cuts from the cooler in his car.

He left his Jeep with a second bag from the trunk. He felt the heft along his shoulder, but he carried the burden until reaching his room. There he laid out the equipment gathered, which included two Sig Sauer pistols, a hunting knife, a Kevlar vest, and a mirror for sightlines. He brought along additional tech as a precautionary measure, including a jammer for the internal feed, which added to his three-minute window. Finally, he took out an access card swiped from a passing attendant during his rounds through the Savery.

All were scattered on the bed farthest from the door. His notes stretched across the small desk beside the bed on a map of the establishment. Each exit was clearly labeled, including those set to the emergency alarm system. He preferred to remain quiet during his stay, but if it came down to it, Lincoln would go out very loud.

Lincoln settled in for the night, his deadline fast approaching. Only he would serve it his way. His mission was vital, the objective the only thing holding him together in this place of the past.

Des Moines stood as a reminder of everything wrong in his life. From the loss suffered within these walls to the death of his mother four states over and two decades earlier, loss was at the heart of his being. Right up to Ruth Heller—the reason for his trip in the first place.

He needed to bury the past, and he would. Right next to the man called the Witness.

Dawn had yet to approach when Lincoln left his room. Kevlar vest in place, twin pistols at his hips, Lincoln set the internal jammer along the back of his door and turned it on. The red recording light on the cameras in view went dark. The jammer offered him a full minute before the cameras returned. He rushed to the end of the hall, pounding into the stairwell in a race for the eleventh floor.

He burst into the hall. The clock continued to count down the seconds. Silent on the lush carpet of the corridor, Lincoln disconnected the closest camera. Brisk steps carried him to the two monitoring the center of the hall, which quickly joined the first.

Lincoln checked his watch. Ten seconds. The camera at the far end of the eleventh floor remained active, the red light flashing. The jammer ran out of juice under its current workload. Lincoln dove for the small wire and unclasped the circuit before his picture ended up being broadcast to the security hub off the lobby.

The three-minute window began.

He didn't need it any longer. Lincoln caught his breath. He carried a single Sig Sauer in his right hand and the keycard in his left.

He approached each room in turn. No lights flowed beneath the doors to any of them until he reached Room 11-10.

Of course.

Lincoln used the keycard. The door eased from the frame under his guiding hand. Gliding along the carpet slowly to minimize noise, Lincoln entered the room. He closed the door without a whisper.

He rounded a slight corner into the suite proper. The curtains were closed to the coming day. The bedroom was tucked to the left along with the bathroom. Both were heavily shadowed and empty.

What mattered was the living area, where a small lamp illuminated the room. Striped wallpaper marked the entire space. Framed photos dotted each wall, and there was a thin green carpet at his feet. A couch and two recliners faced a wall-mounted television, years out of date. On the far side of the room stood a dining table, chairs turned toward the newcomer. Sitting upright in one of the hardwood chairs was a thin man with thick, opaque glasses. He wore a dark suit and red tie. He smiled and lifted a glass of water, showcasing a meal tray at his side filled with eggs, bacon and toast.

Preparation was key to the success of an operation. But preparation meant little to a man who predicted every move before it was made.

"Welcome, Agent MacKenzie," the Witness said. "Can I offer you some breakfast?"

CHAPTER THREE

Coffee tasted sweeter in Styrofoam. There were few facts to support her findings, yet with every sip Morgan Dunleavy grew more and more convinced. The two tablespoons of sugar resting at the base helped as well.

A smile accompanied the beverage, a change from her previous routine. Then again, Morgan's time in Chicago had brought many such changes. Ones she hoped to build upon. Most thought it was due to the upcoming holiday season and the perpetual joy that came from the never-ending shopping, the constant parties, and the get-togethers to commemorate the season.

None of those had effected the change in Morgan. No, Chicago had made the situation plain; her distance had caused their troubles, aided in the abduction of a close colleague, and almost shattered a potential partnership before it formed.

She refused to let that happen again. Instead of protecting her heart, of distancing herself from others, Morgan chose to embrace the people around her.

It was a chance to focus on living for the first time in years; Morgan worked to build rather than sabotage. That fresh attitude cemented her smile, and brought her to the analyst hub on the first floor of the four-story structure in Bethesda.

Karen Cooke was her partner for the moment. The middle-aged investigator with the penchant for Troll dolls on her desk—gifts from her kids as a joke, she said—had started with the department six months earlier. She was a former cop from Utah, and Karen had chosen the quiet life of an analyst rather than the constant red tape of a department willing to look the other way instead of promoting the more-than-qualified woman.

Viewing a crime scene from afar, noticing details from photos rather than being present in the room, took a certain breed. Karen had settled into the position quickly and enjoyed the work, helping to solve a series of murders within her first week.

Early success brought frustration when cases remained in her queue, especially when suspects and clues fell out of reach as they had that morning.

"Wait," Morgan said. "Go back."

Around them, dozens of analysts worked at their stations. They pulled apart cases shuffled over from sister agencies around the country, all in the attempt to find some missing, crucial piece of evidence. Clacking fingers and music blaring from headphones provided background noise to the expansive room, which took up most of the floor. Monitors ran along the walls. The display showed the file numbers currently in work and the analysts assigned to each one. Another monitor listed incoming work and returning cases, hopefully solved and awaiting approval by superiors.

Karen pulled in close to the monitor, her voice low. Morgan enjoyed the woman's company and was glad to join her on the case as she circled the floor. Before Chicago, Morgan had remained locked in the basement, taking assignments as they arrived, never communicating, always willing to forgo sleep. She used to jump at the first sign of field work in the hopes that it would keep her from the company of others. It had taken the frustrating words of Ben Riley, of all people, to shake her from that sensation, and she was grateful for the exchange.

He had offered her a chance to make amends with the talented people surrounding her at the DSA. It was an opportunity she refused to pass up.

"What is it?" Karen asked, mouse scrolling through dozens of open tabs on her desktop.

"There."

Reports shifted along the screen and Morgan's hand fell on the analyst's when it settled on the correct file: a forensics report tinted in green, the location of Mansfield, Texas, noted on the label.

"Why is this in here?"

Karen squinted through a pair of reading glasses as she tucked back her thick tan hair. "Local boys must have thought there was something to it. It's dated three months before the rest."

Three months before a string of murders in Dallas. All the victims had been local women—one per week for the last three. They all shared the same characteristics: blond and Caucasian. All were aged between 25 and 35, and all career women—not the stay-at-home type. Nothing connected the victims, and there were no local businesses where they would cross paths to learn how they were targeted in the first place.

It wasn't the most unusual thing she had seen, not by a long shot. In an all-hands-on-deck situation, it was not unusual to pull in outside consultants to review mounting evidence and field phone calls from local tip lines to corroborate findings from the field. Yet something about the report from Mansfield, just outside the target zone of their killer, gnawed at Morgan's thoughts.

"Strange," she muttered, scanning the file once more.

"Not really," Karen interjected. She settled along her chair and sighed. "Local feds flag items of interest all the time. Anything could be connected to an open investigation, and they rely on us to weed it out. Looks like Kinney was the lead. Thought maybe this was connected to the other victims, but he never had the evidence to pursue. According to this report anyway."

Morgan leaned closer, scanning the images littering the screen. "It's right there."

"Where?"

"Okay," Morgan said, running her tongue over her teeth. She took a breath, tapping lightly on the metal desk of her colleague. "We have three victims in the Dallas area. Certain type. Certain build. Multiple stab wounds to the chest. Same M.O. between them. Another one is missing, so we're on the clock. Now look at this other victim."

Karen's brow furrowed. "Only one stab wound. Boyfriend said it was an intruder. Broken locks on the window corroborated that. He even ended up cut pretty bad on the arm before running the perp out of the place."

"His place."

"Yeah…"

Morgan edged closer. "And he offered little in the way of a description."

"It was dark," Karen replied. "Morgan, if you're suspecting he—"

"Not suspecting at all, actually."

Karen scoffed, then brought up the interview. "He had an alibi when Kinney questioned him for the other murders. He was clean."

"Oh, I'm sure he had a story in place," Morgan said. "What was it? Old flame in town for a visit? Neighbors were over for a dinner party? Who did he pay off to confirm that tall tale?"

Karen laughed, booming through the open room. She covered her lips. "You are way too cynical."

"Born and raised."

"All right," Karen continued. "Where is it, then? The evidence?"

"Right here." Morgan pointed to the images of the boyfriend's apartment.

"I don't see anything."

Morgan waited as Karen squinted over the file. The field agent smiled and tapped the screen. "Incense."

Confusion remained on her colleague's face. Morgan took control of the mouse. She directed the cursor to the file and enlarged the image in question.

Donna Rayburn had been killed by a kitchen knife inside her boyfriend's apartment, the murder weapon taken from the home. By all accounts, she had startled the thief and lost her life for the deed. Forensics had combed the scene, taking photos of every square inch of the apartment, which included a golden bowl kept on a bookshelf—a makeshift altar.

"This incense is used in religious ceremonies," Morgan said. "Including the one described in the Book of Revelation symbolizing the prayers of the saints in heaven."

"What does that have to do with anything?"

Morgan returned to the forensics report. It listed a chemical compound found in the stab wounds of the other victims. Unidentified by local authorities, they were unable to determine the source of the substance. Morgan, however, had recognized the compound, which matched the incense kept at the boyfriend's.

"Holy crap," Karen uttered. "He dipped the blade in the incense."

"A ritual to him," Morgan said.

"He did it."

"There you go." Morgan finished her coffee. Tossing the empty cup into the refuse bin, Morgan paused at the sight of a man skirting through the area in a hurry. Zac Modine rushed between analysts. The small pouch of his gut bounced with his brisk steps. Questions rose as he passed, but he ignored each in turn in his mad dash for the exit.

She tried to catch his attention with a wave, but failed in the attempt. Why she'd waved in the first place surprised her. Everything to do with Zac had felt that way since Chicago. She had almost lost him, her distance and perpetual arguments over the case had allowed their suspect time to abduct him. It never should have happened.

A large part of her aiding the research team with their work lately started because of Zac. It gave her a reason to stay close to him. His presence, even at a distance, brought a smile to her face. It was another mystery, one she hoped to examine in greater detail.

"I can't believe you noticed that," Karen said, pulling her back to the cubicle. She put her notes together for their return trip to the FBI Field Office and what would be a grateful Agent Kinney. She paused. "Religious girl, huh?"

"Me?" Morgan asked as she stood. "Long time ago, but it stopped meaning anything."

"Why?"

"Too cynical, remember?"

Karen nodded. "Still, I appreciate your help."

"You would have seen it."

It was the job. It had never been about glory; it was about saving a potential life. Of building something from nothing, which was where her life had been before the DSA.

Morgan turned to leave. Before she had reached the end of the neighboring cubicle a hand raised for her attention: another analyst hoping for a fresh pair of eyes on a case. Morgan grinned, halfway through a nod when her phone beeped at her hip. She reached for it and pulled the bulky device from her pocket.

SINAI HOSPITAL. ICU.
HE NEEDS YOU.

Sinai Hospital? Baltimore? What could — ?

"I have to go," she said, phone tight against her palm.

"Morgan?" Karen called. "Is everything all right?

"Fine," she said, racing for the end of the row and the exit. "Just fine."

She hoped. Lord, how she hoped it was.

CHAPTER FOUR

Zac waited until the hub was behind him before he took a breath. His cheeks, flushed a deep red, relaxed. His back settled along the wall. Sweat pooled along his phone, nestled tight against his palm.

Did I make the right move?

The simplicity of the job offered a clear answer. When personal matters factored into the decision-making process, things tended to skew to the complicated. Information was his bailiwick, the reason for his position in the office. To share what he could somehow never mattered as much as it did today.

It was the right thing to do.

It was a heavy-handed justification—none of which meant anything to the people around him. Questions surged, even during his distraction, picking at his brain for the procedures and protocols set in place with the daily delivery of cases.

The flow ran through his department. His system allowed the Inter-Agency Council access to the current workload so they could view the timetable and keep pace with the cases funneled their way by their sister agencies.

Zac did his best to answer the questions, to keep checks in place so he could review the work completed by the analysts in the hub. Dozens of men and women, highly qualified investigators, worked through cases sent by other agencies for a fresh set of eyes. Zac's job was simple: offer them any assistance and keep the trains running on time.

Today, he was failing at both. His distraction, the phone in his grip, distanced him from the routine. A routine he had treasured for so long. It had kept him content and sated during his long days in the DSA warehouse.

His time in the Windy City had changed things. Routine had become mundane. Procedures and protocol had turned to limitations of the mind and spirit. Even his home life had shifted. He suddenly found new interests and new desires, none of which he had been quite prepared for or understood.

"Everything all right?"

Zac's head snapped back and collided with the wall. A curse slipped from his lips. His hand ran along the future bump on the back of his skull. He turned to face a young woman in the doorway to the hub.

"Huh? Sorry?"

"Didn't mean to startle you. I was actually talking to you for a full minute before I realized you were spaced out." She stood at his shoulder, an innocent smile on her face. She held a tablet device under her arm, cradling it close.

"You were?"

"Yes."

Zac straightened along the wall, hand to his chest. "Talking to me?"

"Yes, again," she said.

Zac shook his head, blinking hard. "Why was that?"

"Ah," said the bemused woman. "I meant to lead with that. I may have on the first attempt. Alison Adler."

"Zac Modine." He tucked his phone away and wiped the sweat along his pants before offering a handshake.

"I know."

His cheeks were flush. "At least one of us does."

Adler's eyes widened and she chuckled. Her hand fell to her side. "I'm your new partner in Operations."

"My new..." His breath caught in his throat. *How hard did I hit my head against the wall?* "I'm sorry?"

Apparently, Adler failed to recognize his expression or the confusion. "I've been familiarizing myself with the workflow and your procedures since Director Metcalf approached me for the position."

"She did?" First Ben's recruitment without Zac's knowledge and now this? Operations held the DSA together. It was his place to know what was going on; that let him better plan out the day's events should any crisis arise. *His* job and now?

"You're here to do what, again?"

"Assist you," she beamed. Small dimples dotted her cheeks. "I'll be helping the researchers while I'm also working to prep ongoing cases for the field team. Logistics and equipment are my specialties. Very excited to be here."

"I can tell."

Adler peered around the corner at the bustle of the research team. "So where do I—?"

"Are you up to speed on our personnel, our process, everything Operations handles for the department?"

"Up to speed. Yes."

"Huh." No training. No warning of any kind. Who was this woman and what was she really doing here? Nothing made sense to Zac, who glimpsed at his watch and reeled at the sight of the time.

"You okay, Zac?"

"Yeah," he mumbled, rubbing his neck. "No, I'm good. Just distracted today. I thought I might get some fresh air."

"It's twelve degrees outside."

"Can you manage the queue? Handle any questions from the hub?"

Adler hesitated. "You want me to run the workflow?"

He hated the very idea of stepping away, almost as much as he hated the surprise of Adler's presence at the DSA. He didn't require assistance, or a second pair of hands. He handled Operations with efficiency and pride. Her arrival forced him to question that distinction.

"If you're up for it."

"Not... not a problem," she replied. "You sure—?"

"Definitely. Thanks."

Adler entered the hub without a glance back. Zac tracked her movements. She inched down the aisle, hand extended to the staffers as she passed. She was a natural with them. Smiles spread throughout the room at her arrival. That never happened for him.

Zac turned to leave. Thoughts of Adler trailed his steps and he failed to see an older gentleman rounding the corner until it was too late. Both staggered back from the collision. Zac skidded to a halt, eyes panicked at his carelessness.

"Oh," he exclaimed. The man fixed his sweater vest along his chest. "Deputy Director! I didn't see you... hear you, even... Sorry."

Greg Sullivan waited for the muttering to end before offering a smile. "A bit tightly wound this morning, Mr. Modine?"

Morgan passed them in the hall before he could reply. Zac laughed nervously, eyes low to the floor. Unnoticed in her rush, his gaze followed her to the security station at the end of the hall.

"Just a bit too much coffee," he said to the waiting deputy director.

"Not enough sleep," Sullivan finished. "I'm aware of the adage."

Morgan was gone. Another breath escaped, his cheeks burning. Zac ran a hand through his hair. "Can I help you with something?"

"Yes, in fact. I am looking for the most recent reports on the Promethean situation."

"Henry Reed?" Zac asked. Days had passed since Chicago. Days without a word from the man Zac had called friend by the end of their time together. "I mean, everything was uploaded for the Council's review. I did it myself."

"Has there been any follow up to the Bellbrook affair? I understand certain assets have been in play to deal with the fallout?"

An understatement. No answers had come from their time in Ohio. Every inquiry was blocked. The DOD's involvement remained as much a mystery as the event itself.

"Not that I've heard," Zac said. "I can double check if you'd —"

"I'm sure I can handle it," Sullivan answered, a coy smile along his lips.

Procedure dictated that all actions taken by Operations, either in the field or by those in-house, were sent for review up the chain. Sullivan sat in the next link, approving what he could or taking it directly to the Inter-Agency Council for deliberation. From budgetary concerns to personnel to the work at hand, Sullivan had access to it all.

Meaning, his question related to something else entirely, which ramped up Zac's curiosity. The tech settled along the wall once more, trying to get a read on his superior. Then he caught a glimpse of the clock and realized time was slipping away from him.

"If that's all, I should—"

"How are you, Zac?" Sullivan continued, a hand to the tech's arm. "Chicago would have been traumatic for the best of us, I would imagine."

He never should have been in the field. Sent on a dubious intelligence mission, Zac had been faced with an armed wetwork team, a kid who could burst into flames at a whim, an abduction, and multiple murders. Not what he called a winning vacation.

"I... I'm fine. Thank you for asking."

Sullivan nodded. "You are a trusted part of this team, Zac. Your well-being is my utmost priority. I'm sure Susan feels the same."

Metcalf stood down the hall outside her office. A stray glance flitted their way, thin eyes questioning the discussion.

"I would not place a wager on that, sir."

The director of the DSA had remained distant since their chat following his recent assignment. He'd railed against her motivations and she had offered little in the way of defense. It was not her way and he was out of line—tired and mentally drained from the time away. Metcalf had sent him in the field to spy on Ben, the act alone a violation of everything the DSA stood for as an agency.

His comments had divided them on the subject and he'd paid for it since, with the recruitment of a subordinate he didn't need or want.

"Problems with the director?"

"No. I shouldn't have said anything."

"Nonsense," Sullivan said, keeping close to the tech. "We couldn't do this without you, Zac. If something is bothering you I want to know. Both as your superior and as your friend."

"Of course, sir," Zac said, surprised at the compassion offered by the man. He knew little of Sullivan. Even after months of working together, Zac had gleaned scant details about the man. Nothing screamed loyalty from Sullivan, yet here he was offering his trust to the Head of Operational Support and Research. "Thank you. I'm fine. Really."

"I'll leave you to it, then."

Zac nodded and started down the hall. His loafers squeaked

along the tile. They were muted by the deputy director's voice.

"Oh, one last thing."

"Yes?" Zac asked.

Sullivan shuffled close, his voice soft against the murmurs from the rest of the building. "Do you know where Agent MacKenzie is currently?"

"Lincoln?"

Sullivan confirmed with a nod. His hand grazed the beard along his chin. "I've tried to find him, all to no avail. He hasn't logged into the building all week."

"He hasn't?" How had Zac missed that? Sure, Lincoln was never the top concern for Zac, but to fail to notice a field agent had gone missing? "Are there any operations currently—"

"None on the books as far as I know," Sullivan said. "But you're the man to see about that, aren't you? Susan never puts an operation on the board without you, does she?"

Protocol demanded it that way. It provided oversight and protection for the assets in the field. The constant review kept the agency safe against control from outside agendas. That was how it was meant to be, anyway. Yet Metcalf had failed to follow such guidelines multiple times in recent days and it gave Zac pause.

"She—"

"So where is Lincoln MacKenzie?" Sullivan interrupted, pressing over Zac's muttering.

"I don't know."

Sullivan scratched his beard and looked down the hall. Zac followed suit, standing close to the man. Outside her office, Susan Metcalf met with a woman, another stranger to the building. Thin black hair covered her features, and a gaunt profile hid deep green eyes.

"Don't you find that odd, Zac?" Sullivan whispered as Metcalf and the woman slipped from view, their conversation hidden from the rest of the department. "It's almost like you've been kept out of it on purpose. But why would Susan do that? Doesn't she trust you?"

CHAPTER FIVE

Ben Riley needed a car. Something with some pep, maybe with some flames decorating the side. Fancy rims and a speaker system in the trunk would announce his arrival, most likely blasting 90s pop rock as a greeting.

It was thoughts like those that distracted Ben from the mildew scent filtered throughout the transit bus. Though it was a necessary evil for transportation, Ben found more and more desire for a ride of his own.

A DeLorean would have been nice, a bumper sticker reading *88mph or Bust* on the back.

Instead, he traveled at twenty or below for the majority of his trek from his Edgemont apartment to a stop three blocks from the DSA warehouse. A car was definitely in the cards at some point. For now, however, the bus came with distinct advantages.

First and foremost was the visibility factor, especially considering the surveillance tracking his every move. They had continued, the suited men from the mall. Despite changing his daily habits in the aftermath of his failed attempt to contact Emily Wright, they continued watching him during his off hours. They followed him to work. They tracked him as soon as he left the compound in downtown Bethesda. Grocery shopping. The movies. Everything was fair game to them.

Ben said nothing—never gave them a second glance. What he did do, though, was keep his service weapon on him at all times. The Ruger holstered beneath his jacket comforted him.

When his call for assistance had failed—when he'd realized a target had been placed on Emily's back thanks to his mounting fear—he waited for the fallout. Waited for them to converge on his position, to strip him of the new life he had barely begun to understand.

They never came. No new bugs were planted in his apartment—none he was able to locate, anyway. Nothing was said at work. None of the multiple parties mentioned by his last-minute savior in the mall came forward with their plans. It left Ben frustrated and wary.

And incredibly nervous.

A sedan parked at his bus stop justified the sensation. He had noted the car two blocks from the stop, eyes constantly scanning the traffic patterns from his regular window seat on the bus. Two men waited outside the navy blue Ford, leaning against the cold frame, gaze locked on the approaching bus.

"Oh, this can't be good."

Ben jumped to his feet, his neighbor startled by the sudden move. The agent attempted a quick egress, though he was blocked by the elderly man at his side.

"What are you—?"

"Excuse me, please."

Unable to sneak past the man, who was too confused to react with any speed, Ben hoisted his legs over the passenger and used the vacant seat in front of them to escape. Ben rushed for the front of the bus, catching the driver in the mirror overhead.

"Sir, please take your seat," the driver declared with wide eyes. "We'll be at the next stop in a minute."

"Part of my problem," Ben replied without pause. "Open the door."

"When we get to the stop."

"Now." He flipped his badge open, then pointed to the controls. "Open the door now."

The driver shook his head and slammed on the brakes. A block out from the stop, stuck in the middle of the intersection as the light changed to red, the hulking behemoth squealed to a halt. Ben snatched a nearby pole for support as he almost tumbled into the dashboard.

The doors opened and he was out on the street before they finished. Ben did not pause, did not hesitate. He broke into a full run away from the waiting stop. Horns blared, and waiting traffic poured into the intersection. None overpowered the bellowing tones of the two men waiting at the bus stop.

"He's making a run for it!"

His partner slammed off the car to give chase. "I told you we should have waited in the damn car!"

"Cut him off," the other shouted. "Go!"

Both pursued the fleeing agent. Their path headed away from the DSA warehouse. Ben had no plan, no destination in mind, other than ditching the two suits. Who they were, and what their intentions might be, were afterthoughts when it came to his survival.

Cars screeched to a halt as Ben crossed the street. He dodged the first, then hopped over the hood of the second as all awaited the changing light. He needed distance, time to consider what the hell was going on and what his next step might be.

He needed help.

Rounding the corner, Ben continued to run. His phone slipped into his hand, the winter air fogging up the screen as he dialed.

"This is Morgan. Leave a short one, wouldja?"

Ben cursed, and he turned off the phone. Morgan was a last resort, and he counted on their growing partnership more than he cared to admit. Since their last assignment he had gone out of his way to make time for her, to keep the contact growing in the hopes of trusting her with what was happening.

Part of him accepted the lack of response as a blessing. If she had answered, what could he say? What did he actually know? Someone was tracking him—multiple parties, according to a stranger intent on keeping him safe from his surveillance. Any story shared brought danger to Morgan. Emily was already in their crosshairs thanks to him. He couldn't do that to another friend.

This was on him and he had to deal with it. Directly, if need be.

Ben skirted into a local alley off Brookway, four blocks south from the start of his run. His chest was heaving, and the December wind burned his lungs. He tucked tight to the brick of the building, utilizing the deep shadows of the cramped space. His Ruger rested against his palm.

Slow breaths calmed his nerves. The traffic fell to background noise under the pounding steps approaching. Ben peered out of the small inlet of the alley to see a short Caucasian man with a black winter hat over his head and ears, and annoyance in his eyes.

"Dammit," the man muttered. He searched the alley, his pace brisk — too brisk as he missed the tiny inlet within the space.

Ben waited for the man to pass before exiting. "Don't move."

The man stopped. He raised his hands in response. One slowly left the open space above his head for the confines of his jacket. "I'm reaching for my badge."

Ben shook his head, unwilling to take the chance. "I don't think so."

He grabbed the man's shoulder and spun him around. His right hand delivered a crushing blow to the man's left cheek, the impact bolstered by the pistol locked in Ben's grip. His target fell, a small billfold falling from his open hand as he collapsed in the alley.

His badge. Not a gun.

Ben started for the fallen identification, but froze when he heard the click of a weapon behind him.

"That was unnecessary," the second figure said. Ben closed his eyes, locking the safety on his Ruger. He lowered it slowly, and then let the weapon clatter against the pavement. "Now kick it away."

The gun skittered to the far side of the alley and past the groaning man. Ben remained in position, hands outstretched and passive.

"You all right, Martin?" the man behind him called. The aching figure rolled to his side. A hand swiped the trickle of blood at the back of his skull. Martin worked his way to his feet, eyes blinking rapidly to focus.

"Bastard sucker punched me, Kanigher. What do you think?"

Kanigher's gun poked Ben in the back. "Not the brightest move, Riley."

Ben shook his head. He refused to give an inch or close his eyes. "Just get it over with."

He waited in silence, the gun pressed tight to his back. His eyes locked on Martin, who retrieved his badge and Ben's gun from the ground. Every movement seemed to cause the short man pain.

The pressure along his back subsided as Kanigher's holster welcomed the weapon with a snap. Martin handed Ben his

Ruger back before flipping open his badge.

Ben accepted the gun, confused at the events unfolding. "You're NSA?"

Martin nodded. "You've been requested by the Inter-Agency Council."

The Council? They oversaw the DSA and regulated the agency's function in the field. In his two months in the department he had yet to meet a single member of the Council or been bothered with the political aspects of their mandate.

"Me? Why?"

Martin patted his head. Irritation rose, and he snatched Ben's arm, pulling him forward to their waiting car. "Evaluation, Agent Riley. And right now? I'd be very concerned about your future with the DSA."

CHAPTER SIX
Afghanistan - 2007

He wasn't built for war. The sole thought crossed Lincoln's mind when he entered the encampment four klicks outside Lashkar Gah. It wasn't his own shortcomings that gave the seasoned Sergeant Major of the US Army pause. Lincoln was in his third tour in the heart of the fight against terrorism. No, the thought was directed at the newest recruit that had been assigned to his unit.

"Specialist Marcus Engers?"

"Your new sniper," Captain Franklin Thomas replied. The captain was a hard man, born and raised in war from the four generations that preceded him and lived to tell the tale. Lincoln respected him and knew better than to question orders. Lincoln understood the chain of command, and appreciated the fact that Thomas spoke to him as an equal with decisions that came across his desk rather than simply barking nonsense for the sake of his rank.

Still, Lincoln looked to him curiously. "Sir? We don't need a new sniper. Ford is—"

"I know, Sergeant." Thomas walked quicker through the makeshift barracks to the north of Sangin. The siege was over for the most part, small pockets of resistance being brought down almost hourly. "Ford isn't going anywhere. He's getting a playmate."

Both stopped at the outskirts of the barracks. A gangly boy stood proudly in front of a group of reporters that had been embedded in the camp to report on the conflict. He smiled and Lincoln could see the whites still in place. There was no sand caked to the front of his teeth. He was fresh to the fight.

"Wait," Lincoln said, staring at his new recruit. "Engers?"

Thomas nodded. "Senator's kid."

"He enlisted?"

"Course he did," Thomas said with a huff. "On camera no less. Your next assignment is little more than a photo op to him. I hear he plans on following his old man right into the political limelight. Now he's ours to babysit. Well, yours."

The assignment took them south of Lashkar Gah. Intelligence came from contacts within the Mossad—Israeli Intelligence—and was verified through a number of official channels until it came to the desk of Captain Thomas and Lincoln's squad. A low-level operative with the Taliban had been sighted in the region. Naseem Qir. Reports suggested Qir had vital information for the International Security Assistance Force's effort.

In truth, Qir offered little as an asset. He was merely a potential headline to appease the people back home. The bigger goal was to show off a possible hero in the form of the twenty-year-old Marcus Engers. The future of politics was at stake, supposedly.

Qir had gone to ground years earlier after a series of attacks in France. The Mossad had been able to discover his weak spot. Qir had only come up for air between missions for a woman he called his daughter, though not by blood. She was a surrogate for the family he'd lost to violence a decade earlier. She resided in a small outcropping of makeshift buildings south of the city. The settlement had most likely sprung up out of necessity from the innocents fleeing the war zones across the country.

The team's official goal was clear. Bring in Qir. Alive.

Typically, his squad handled high-priority targets. They dealt with current threats to national security, the kind no one ever found out about. Lincoln's squad of six—now seven—prevented potential tragedies from getting off the ground by taking out the minds behind them.

Lincoln led the assault. From his team, he brought Dietrich and Vogel with him. Both had been recruited for the squad directly and had earned their place on the front line time and again. Carmichael and Nolan remained with the Humvee for exfil. The final two members of the squad, Ford and Marcus, took positions on the outskirts of the city for cover fire.

"Take a breath, Engers." Lincoln inched down the street of the makeshift city. *City* was a stretch of the definition, of course. Three roads ran the length of the outcropping of tents and thinly constructed huts that encompassed the center of the settlement. Those built along the outskirts were made of heavy stone, all fairly small due to the lack of material, though they were enough to give a perfect view of the horizon in case of invaders. Or, in the case of Lincoln's team, they provided a perfect vantage point to see the settlement in its entirety.

"Sir?" the recruit asked, confused.

"You're breathing into the line," Lincoln whispered, continuing toward the large domicile in the center of the village. They crept along the thin strip between buildings and scanned the area. No one was around. It made them uneasy. "We don't need the attention."

"Oh. Damn. Right."

"Muttering isn't helpful either. Any signs of life?"

"No, sir," Marcus started before cutting off for a brief pause. "I mean, I thought I..."

"Make it clear, Engers. Yes or no?" Lincoln stopped in front of their target. Dietrich and Vogel moved to either side of the front door.

"No," Marcus confirmed.

"Clear on my end too, sir," Ford relayed with clear agitation. "Thanks for asking."

Lincoln rolled his eyes. Ford's obnoxious behavior about the new addition had started with a tantrum at the morning briefing. Lincoln had put an end to it, though some still bled through his earpiece.

Dietrich chuckled, pressed tight against the front wall of the home. "Sounds jealous of the pretty boy, boss."

"Stow the chatter. We're here." Lincoln moved in front of the door. "Kid, I said we're here."

"Me?"

Lincoln crooked his head and gritted his teeth. Vogel nodded to him. "Call the play, new guy. I don't feel like dying here."

"Right. Sorry." Another brief pause. Lincoln felt sweat pooling from the dry heat even in the middle of the night. "You're clear. Proceed."

"Gladly," Lincoln said. He eased the door open. Vogel and

Dietrich were in the domicile before Lincoln's next breath, the pair scanning their respective sides of the home.

They were greeted with nothing. Emptiness. No Naseem Qir. No surrogate daughter. Not even the appearance of a home for them. No furniture. No dishes. Nothing.

A set up. Lights flashed through the windows of the faux domicile. The three men circled back to the road, catching torchlight bearing down on them from all sides.

"Oh, hell." Lincoln pulled his colleagues across the strip. "We're blown."

"You think?" Dietrich said. The thin street of the village filled with men traveling in packs. Each carried a Kalashnikov automatic rifle, out-of-date models easily purchased from a dozen local vendors looking to arm their own people against the oppressors in their midst. Lincoln ducked between two buildings. Vogel laid down fire to cover their retreat.

"Engers," Lincoln yelled through the comm line over the sound of gunfire. "We need a clear line out!"

"Mack!"

Lincoln turned as Vogel jumped in front of him. Three shots slammed into the man's chest, ripping through his body armor like tissue paper. Lincoln watched John Vogel fall, his vacant eyes staring at the stars above.

The sergeant major tried to catch him, tried to pull him back to his feet as if nothing had happened. Before he could reach the dead man lying in the sand, Dietrich had grabbed his arm and pulled him farther into the village, away from the rushing lights of their attackers.

Lincoln screamed, dropping four men in a spray of bullets, which gave the remaining pair time to put some distance between them and the ambush. Across the settlement, Lincoln heard sniper fire from Ford's position. A dozen shots echoed in the chasms between homes. Then there was nothing but silence.

"Ford?"

No answer chirped through the radio. Stray shots echoed along the streets. Lincoln started for Ford's last location. He made it three steps before Dietrich stopped him.

"Linc," the man whispered. He pulled him down and pointed ahead. Lights ran up and down the streets. Multiple targets blocked any clear path to Ford. "He's out of reach. If he's even—

"

"We can't just leave him."

The lights shifted and caught their presence. Dietrich fired while pushing Lincoln away from the approaching threat. "No choice, Linc. Move!"

"Carmichael," Lincoln called through the comm. "We need exfil. Now. Coming in hot to the south."

"On our way," the deep voice of the woman replied.

"South, people," Lincoln ordered. "Make for the ridge at exfil point alpha."

Dietrich led them to the outskirts of the village and the position of Marcus Engers. "So much for the milk—"

Dietrich fell without a sound, blood vacating his now lifeless form through a small hole in his neck. Lincoln stared at his friend's body for a long moment in disbelief. He wanted to pull at him, to drag him up on his feet and force him to continue. To demand another joke and to hear the bravado he needed to make it through.

Roger Dietrich was gone. Lincoln took one last look, then blitzed into the corridor, taking out Dietrich's murderer with a single shot to the head before slipping into the shadows once more. He crossed three small homes in an instant. Short bursts of gunfire kept his pursuers at bay.

At the edge of town he paused. Exfil was less than a minute out, but he knew there was one objective he had yet to fulfill. Qir was a lost cause. Marcus, though, remained a viable asset. He was the public face of the unit now—their hero in waiting, no matter what Lincoln thought of his performance.

Lincoln found the rope that led to the roof of the southernmost point of the village and ascended. His feet hit the ground and he stayed low, creeping across the roof. Marcus was frozen on the far side of the building, head tucked and eyes closed. He failed to see the insurgent making his way over, a knife in his hand.

Two shots dropped him, causing Marcus to spin around. "Sir?"

"Move your ass, kid!" Lincoln yanked him to his feet and the two raced back down the ladder. Droves of footsteps came from behind them. They rushed into the expanse of desert. No cover. No more time. Lincoln focused on the surviving member of his team by his side. He focused on his breathing.

He waited for an end that never came.

Lincoln and Marcus fell to their knees when Carmichael and the Humvee crested the nearest dune. The M2 Browning atop the vehicle, manned by Nolan, laid waste to the insurgents at Lincoln's back. Lincoln pulled at Marcus, dragging him toward the Humvee with everything he had left.

"Go! Go!"

Carmichael helped them inside before shifting back into position. The Humvee whirled away from the scene, Nolan covering their rear. Few shots followed them into the night. No more were needed. Lincoln kept his head low as he caught his breath. The faces of Vogel and Dietrich plagued his thoughts. And then there was Ford. He never had the chance to find Ford.

"Sir?" A hand rested on his shoulder. Tears filled Marcus' eyes. "I don't know what to say. I—"

"Then don't," Lincoln snapped, pushing away from the kid. He regretted it immediately, seeing the fear in Marcus' eyes. He regretted it, though he'd meant it nonetheless.

Marcus wasn't built for war. None of them should have been. For Marcus, though, Lincoln could tell his time deep in the trenches against the enemy was over. In that moment, Lincoln wasn't sure if he hated the kid or envied him.

CHAPTER SEVEN

"Don't move a muscle, you son of a bitch."

Lincoln edged into the room, fingers tense along the grip of the Sig Sauer. He tapped lightly along the trigger. It could have ended right then and there. Confirmation of the target, one bullet, and mission accomplished. Instead, Lincoln scanned the room, weapon leveled on the Witness, who smirked with devilish pride.

"Not a muscle?" he asked coyly. "I'd prefer to keep this water from spilling, but if it makes you feel threatened we can chalk it up to a housekeeping error. Not a stretch for this staff, trust me on that. You have seen the so-called duck-shaped towels at the end of the bed? Of course you have. How was your stay in room 327? Did you get a good night's sleep?"

All Lincoln's preparation had been for naught. The moment he'd arrived he was locked into this confrontation, one foreseen somehow on every level by the man sitting comfortably in his chair. The Witness tipped his glass closer to his lips. Lincoln clenched tighter along the grip of the sidearm in frustration.

"Finished?" Lincoln asked.

"That depends on your trigger finger, I would imagine. Is that a correct assessment, Agent MacKenzie?"

"That's enough of that too."

"You prefer Lincoln?"

The Witness lowered the glass. It clattered against the tray, settling next to the still-steaming tray of eggs, bacon and toast.

"If you've got something other than the Witness for yourself."

"Clever," the Witness said. "Agent it is."

"You seem pretty calm for a man facing the barrel of a gun."

"Is that what I'm doing? I believed I was facing the bereaved boyfriend of one Ruth Heller."

Lincoln rushed him, fire in his eyes. Red surrounded everything, the blood pumping harder through his veins. He slammed his fist against the breakfast tray. It crashed to the floor with a clang, sending the contents flying across the carpet. Lincoln reached for the Witness, the gun pressed tight to the man's neck.

"You must be damn stupid to even *think* her name."

The Witness' eyes were blocked by the opaque lenses of his glasses, but in the dim light afforded by the lamp Lincoln thought he noticed a glow emanating, burning brighter with every word spoken.

Ruth's name had sent him into a rage, and he fought to keep his temper in check. Struggling to catch his breath, he tried to remember their last words together, their last joke shared, their last fight. All he could hear from his fading memory was silence.

"Perhaps," the Witness breathed, cool and collected. His hand slowly brushed the sidearm away from his person. Lincoln let the pistol drop to his side as he backed away. "I am here, after all. Yes, your so-called quest to track me down was very well placed, but I thought I would help it along. And why not here? Your great failure. Where did the senator meet his end? Was it here?"

The eggs stuck to the carpet, the bacon scattered like burnt flesh. Lincoln tried to focus on the breakfast, but could only see the past. The dead man he had failed to protect. The moment he had lost everything.

"Perhaps the mess would do some good, then," the Witness continued. "I'm sure there's still some trace of the man here."

"Stop," Lincoln seethed, gripping the closest recliner for support. "Stop talking."

"Ah, I forgot. You were sent to, how was it put again? To end me?"

Those had been Metcalf's exact words—her orders, down to the slightest of inflection in the man's voice. It was as if he'd stood in the room next to them, watching with glee at the hate in their eyes. He appeared almost content with their vindictive hunt for him after his actions in Bellbrook.

"How could you possibly know that?"

"That. This event. Your time in Afghanistan. Even your mother's death. Information is there for all to see. Simple facts to discern if one possesses the foresight." The Witness laughed. Beside him, resting on the neighboring chair, was an overturned notecard. His hand grazed the object thoughtfully, which drew Lincoln's attention. The irritated agent moved for it.

"You're not ready for this yet," the Witness said. His hand clamped tight over the card.

"Then tell me. Why Bellbrook? Why Ruth?"

"No, Lincoln," the Witness said with the wag of his finger. "Sorry. Agent. But no. *That's* not what you want to ask."

"Yes, it is."

"Have you thought of her since her death? Her scent? Her touch? Her smile, if she had one? What attracted you to her? How has your life truly changed with her loss? Can you answer any of that?"

Lincoln fell silent. He'd met Ruth two years ago on a routine case with the DSA field team. She was new to the unit, her experience coming from the cyber side of warfare. He had saved her that day, and she had thanked him. What had he saved her from? He couldn't recall.

Neither could he picture her face, nor how it had changed in their two years of friendship and the last few weeks of something much deeper. They had both needed something more in the wake of Grissom's demise and found each other.

Who had made the first move? What line had it been that ended with them sharing a bed? That was another detail, like the color of her eyes or the way her hair fell, that had slipped from memory—erased and replaced to make room for his revenge.

The Witness read his disdain for the question. "No. You can't, can you? Not you. You used her and are *still* using her."

"Shut up," Lincoln spat. The gun returned, shaky in his grasp but still steady enough to finish the job.

"Right. The 'ending me' part. Except that isn't what you want."

He fought against the man's words and against his own trepidation over the mission. The Witness had killed seven thousand people in Bellbrook. This wasn't about revenge, but that was the first step for Lincoln. He needed closure: to do right by Ruth for not being there for her at the end.

He should have been the one to enter that damn forest, not her. Not with the headaches she had presented hours before her death. Lincoln had known she wouldn't be coming back, and he hadn't said a damn thing to stop her. He had made no move to tell her how he felt.

Now he didn't understand what she meant to him or how he felt about any of it. Killing the Witness took over. It was meant to be a righteous blow for justice, but something about the mission didn't sit well with him. He was a soldier serving something bigger—something better than himself. He was not a gun for hire.

"You have no idea what I want," Lincoln replied.

"Believe what you may, Agent. Maybe the old you—the soldier—would have savored the revenge. Ever the great protector, always worried for others.

"Here and now, though? You're not that person. All the hate and bile you've swallowed? You truly believe this to be righteous vengeance. That your actions are justified for a situation you do not understand in the slightest. If you'd take a moment, though, you could achieve so much more with this exchange."

"What the hell are you talking about?"

"An offer," the Witness said with the wave of his hand. "My first being the chair."

"Pass."

"On what? You don't even know. Your training still refuses to let you listen, to see what I can give you."

Lincoln leveled his Sig Sauer on the man. "I know *exactly* what you can give me."

"Answers, Lincoln," the Witness said, light glimmering beneath his glasses. "Answers."

"Call them what they truly are," Lincoln spat in response. "Lies."

"Never," the Witness said. "I can give you every answer you seek. Not only the truth about what happened to Bellbrook and Ruth. I won't deny my hand in that. But there is so much more I can tell you."

"You can't—"

"That is not the end of it, Lincoln. I can offer you so much more. The truth behind the senator's death, for example. The DSA. Everything."

Lincoln hesitated. He kicked at the crumbs on the floor that defiled the spot where a great man fell. The shooter was never found, yet somehow the Witness had uncovered the hidden details of a day that continued to haunt the man. Lincoln hesitated, dreaming of the answers to everything that had gone wrong in his life. From the death of his mother to those lost at his side overseas. From the senator to Grissom to Ruth and every other name etched on a plaque in the basement of the DSA warehouse. Answers to his life, held by a killer, a man Lincoln had been sent to murder.

Lincoln hesitated, and the Witness seemed to recognize the conflict within. "This offer won't last forever, Agent MacKenzie. There is a ticking clock on our meeting, I'm afraid. I'll need your answer now."

"Then I say—"

"Don't," the Witness said, halting his response. "Don't jump at your first instinct. I am offering you everything you've been questioning since Ruth. Ever since your stay at the hospital. What are you fighting for? Do you recall asking that?"

He did. When he had sat with Morgan and her stupid flowers to wish him well, he'd questioned the DSA and their role. It didn't mean the same thing anymore. What was he serving through his actions at the department? Only death? Or was it possible to change his future?

"I can give you answers, Lincoln," the Witness said. "Right here, right now. All you have to do is sit."

CHAPTER EIGHT

The car stopped at the gate of Fort Meade. Soldiers scanned the vehicle as the attendant matched Kanigher's badge to their records. Routine, yet the amount of care for each vehicle entering the massive complex gave the affair a feeling of importance.

Ben said nothing on the drive through Bethesda. Not a joke or a sarcastic witticism regarding the two men casually escorting him to the home of the National Security Agency.

He never should have been there. It was a thought not directed at his current situation, but more about failing to belong anywhere near the widening world of the DSA. The feeling had grown ever since his recruitment, that sense of being out of place. He didn't fit the mold of a field agent. Ben was a cop, mediocre even in that profession, a small fish living comfortably in his miniscule pond.

Bellbrook opened his eyes to an entirely different world. A case unlike any he had witnessed, nothing like what his father's daily lectures had prepared him for. Chicago offered more of the same, though he had done his best to grow into the role.

None of that compared to the awe of seeing Fort Meade. Soldiers patrolled the grounds. Personnel worked proudly to keep the entire nation safe, all without a need for distinction or reward. Now he had been called before them to prove his worth.

After being approved for entry, the car continued through the grounds for the building to the front of the enormous complex. Kanigher tucked his badge into his pocket. Martin rubbed at his wound, his skin already bruising.

"How does it look?"

"Barely noticeable," Kanigher said without a glance to his

partner.

Martin brought down the overhead mirror. His left side was an enormous welt from where Ben's fist had connected, and a bump pulsed at the touch along the back of his skull from his collision with the pavement.

"Barely noticeable?" Martin shouted. "You call *that* barely noticeable? I look like I grew a second head."

"Consider it an improvement," Ben chuckled. "Maybe the second one will turn out better than the first."

The car halted at the sound of their passenger's voice in the back seat. Kanigher and Martin turned around slowly. Ben shrank against the cushion. The words had slipped out, a delayed reaction from not speaking for so long. Not to say it wasn't an accurate assessment. The timing, however, could have been better.

"No one asked you," Martin snapped. Kanigher returned his focus to the drive, coasting through the lot for the empty spot at the end of the row before putting the car in park.

The agents vacated, doors slamming behind them. After losing a swift game of Rock, Paper, Scissors demanded by the obstinate Martin, Kanigher was forced to open the rear driver's side door for their passenger. His aggravation did little to soothe the uncertainty felt by the wary DSA agent. Ben walked closely between them as they entered the stronghold of the NSA.

"Why the secrecy?" Ben asked, passing through the glass lobby for a wide corridor leading deeper into the complex. "Why pick me up at the bus stop instead of at the DSA?"

"Orders."

Ben stopped, and Kanigher nearly plowed into him. Martin continued for a step, then waited. He threw a disarming smile to the questioning stares at seeing the purple welt on his left side.

"Keep moving."

Ben shook his head. "I'd like some orders of my own. Let me contact my superiors to verify this little trip."

"Not going to happen," Kanigher said, prodding him forward.

The frustrated DSA agent staggered a step, then held his ground. "Well, do you know if this counts as a sick day? Personal day? I want to keep accurate track in the paid-time-off system. You know how those bean counters can be if you try to cheat them out of workable hours."

"It's a meeting, Riley," Kanigher said between clenched teeth. "Answer the questions and go home. Simple as that."

The pair continued, not caring for their stubborn passenger any longer. Ben hesitated. "I would have appreciated a call ahead of time. Maybe a limo service to pick me up? Arriving at Fort Meade in style would have been more pleasant than two suits stalking me at a bus stop."

Martin's fist tightened against his side. "Like we don't have more important things to do than handhold the DSA?"

"Not this again," Kanigher sighed.

"You know it's true. Nothing but a bunch of screw ups in that place. Whole damn department needs dismantling," Martin said.

"Tell me how you really feel," Ben said.

"Not me, Riley," Martin said with a smile. They stopped before a pair of white doors. The agents each took a handle, opening to the conference room beyond. "But *they* certainly will."

Ben shuffled into the darkened room. Eyes struggling to focus from the lack of light, Ben returned to the doors. The boom of the frame echoed as they closed.

A table stretched across the length of the room. Thin overhead bulbs hung down from the ceiling and offered small cones of light against the cherry surface. Figures sat patiently at the far end—three women and four men, their features heavily shadowed.

Only one stood out at the head of the table: a large man, tall and proud. Thick hair attempted to cover his bulging forehead; his cheeks were full with rosy jowls. His hands were folded before him, as if he contained the world between his thick digits.

"Have a seat, Agent Riley," the figure said.

"I don't mind standing."

"The chair at the end will work well for you," the man replied. "Would you care for a glass of water?"

Ben pulled the chair out from the table and sat. "A smoothie would be better. Something tropical?"

One of the shadowed figures at the table reached for the pitcher of water in the center of their assemblage. A small glass joined it in his hands as he stood and approached the newcomer to the meeting. Without a glance in Ben's direction, the man put the items in front of Ben then returned to his position.

"Or water is fine," Ben muttered. "Thanks."

There was no eye contact from the others in the room. No reaction to his snide remarks. Nothing to indicate their reason for the meeting, for pulling him from his work. They simply sat, heads lowered, while the figure at the head loomed over them.

"Agent Riley—"

"Call me Ben. I mean, since we're such good friends here."

"Donald Stallworth," the man said, hand to his chest. "I represent the National Security Agency's interests in the DSA's operational status." The door behind Ben shifted open, allowing a stream of light to cut through the room. Stallworth smiled. "And I believe you know my colleague."

Greg Sullivan briskly entered, thick files tucked under his arm. A sharp nod greeted Ben before the deputy director continued to the far side, where he handed over his work to Stallworth.

"And I believe we will keep it as Assistant Director Stallworth and Agent Riley for these proceedings," Stallworth said.

"Got it," Ben replied. "And proceedings is a euphemism for—?"

"Agent Riley," Sullivan called, returning to the center of the chamber. Hands behind his back, sweater vest perfectly ironed, the deputy director approached his subordinate with a disarming smirk. "If you could curb your standard inclination of making an ass of yourself, we might be able to get through this hearing quickly and quietly."

"Without my direct superior or any form of advocate on this side of the table? Unless that's where you come in, Deputy Director?"

Sullivan filled the glass from the pitcher. He placed it before the waiting agent and leaned close. "I'm sure an advocate isn't necessary for this, Agent."

"I'd rather be the judge of that, Greg. But where are my manners?" Ben took a small sip, then smacked his lips loudly. He leaned into his chair and offered the floor to the figure at the far end of the room. "I believe you were about to pass judgment on my actions?"

Stallworth grumbled. Aggravated, he straightened his tie to the knot around his neck. He nodded to the woman to his left, who then reached for the recorder in the center of the table.

"For the record."

"I'd love a copy when we're done," Ben said. "Might have found the cure for my insomnia."

Sullivan cleared his throat. The slight interruption offered a clean break for the recorder, and caused Ben to smile. Not knowing what was coming was one thing, but taking it in silence had never been an option. It was something both prominent figures in the conference room were rapidly discovering.

Stallworth recovered, frustration masked under his thundering voice. "This meeting has been called for the assessment of Agent Benjamin Harrison Riley. Proceedings are in place to determine his viability to the covert agency known as the DSA."

CHAPTER NINE

It was a good week. Clearance rates were on the rise in the analyst hub. The field team had managed a successful extraction in Chicago, despite the lingering questions left from the case. The annual budget-approval process involved less negotiating than previous years, the Inter-Agency Council agreeing to most of the line items on the list.

Yet something worried Susan Metcalf. It may have been a shift in the air, possibly the ever-encroaching new year on the horizon, but something gnawed just beneath the surface. The sensation gave her pause. Or maybe it was seeing Zac talking directly to Sullivan. Ever since Zac's return from Chicago, tensions had risen between them. Sending him to spy on Ben had been necessary. She had needed the information gleaned from the young tech—a chance to see if she had been right in bringing their new agent into the fold.

Zac questioned the objective, questioned every decision of late. She let him—not that her answer was forthcoming. Zac played a role, a vital one, but never to the degree he'd demanded of late. Metcalf had offered him nothing in return for his years of service.

However, seeing him in deep discussion with Sullivan troubled her. The elder statesman of the department had worked in mysterious ways of late. His presence had set a new tone within the Bethesda warehouse, and his inexperience threatened to compromise their protocols at all turns.

The arrival of the woman seated across from her was the latest case in point.

"I was surprised to see your file come across my desk, Agent

Winslow," Metcalf said.

Abigail Winslow, seven-year veteran with the FBI. She sat, legs crossed, her recessed green eyes wide and her pink lips pursed. Thin strands of black hair fell evenly along the sides, tucked behind her ears.

She was the latest recruit to the DSA Field Team according to the report from the Inter-Agency Council. There was only one problem with that filing: Metcalf had never approved it. She had never vetted Winslow, never even held a discussion for bringing a new agent to the team — even though she'd pored over dossiers in the aftermath of Bellbrook. She had held back, unsure of her next move.

It turned out Greg Sullivan had made one of his own in her stead.

"Deputy Director Sullivan approached me with the opportunity. He thought I would be a perfect fit with the team and the agency."

His involvement in personnel only added to her unease. Sullivan had never expressed interest previously. And why, despite his increased presence in the building, had he failed to mention the new member to their happy family. Or the fact that he had gone over her head for the mysterious woman's approval.

Metcalf forced a smile. "Greg is a good judge of character. Typically, however, personnel selection falls to me."

"I see." Winslow's words offered little in the way of character. Her eyes told another tale, however — cold and calculating.

"At ease," Metcalf chided. "This isn't where we part ways. I simply found it interesting an experienced agent with the FBI would jump into a different branch knowing nothing of our mandate."

Winslow grinned, brushing back a handful of stray hairs. "My work with the Bureau was, how do I put this? Boring."

"This isn't the *Impossible Missions Force*, Agent."

Winslow laughed. "No, I know. I do. There's a flexibility here, from what the deputy director mentioned, anyway, that I found much more appealing than my previous position."

Internal alarm bells blared. What details had been shared with this unknown commodity? How much classified information had slipped from the confines of their agency to the newcomer without proper vetting? Sullivan continued to push against established protocol, yet Metcalf couldn't help but feel as though the worst was to come.

Jaw clenched, Metcalf held tight to her growing anxiety. The reports, accumulated from a frantic overnight search for everything containing Winslow's name, covered her desk. Arrest records sat atop commendations, which rested beside psychiatric evaluations from routine sessions. Every search had failed to ease her worries, the information lackluster or outright missing. There was no history beyond her time with the FBI with Winslow, not even any recruitment files from the Bureau. She had merely *appeared* on the server one day; it was almost as if Abigail Winslow didn't exist until seven years ago.

"Let's talk about your casework, then," the director started. "I have only been able to access a smattering of files with your signature on them. Case reports. Assessments. Recommendations. I assumed someone with your experience would have more of a paper trail to offer insight into your tactics. Your operational acumen, so to speak."

"I understand, Director," Winslow replied. She leaned closer to the desk to look over the files. A coy smile broke through. "Most of my cases were classified or are open investigations and cannot be shared at this time."

It was a convenient truth—one unable to be disputed by the frustrated director. Metcalf certainly understood the need for secrets. Winslow, however, was an agent for years with a caseload to match. Yet nothing present in Metcalf's findings, frantic as they might have been due to the less-than-forthcoming nature of Sullivan, allowed the seasoned administrator to contradict the recruit.

"Right," she said, pushing the majority of files aside. One settled to the top and she held firm. "Like the Cooper Massacre?"

"A mess," Winslow said, comfortable in her chair.

"So no suspects?"

"Between you, me, and these walls?" Winslow said with a smirk. "There were loads of suspects. One for every dollar held in the Cooper family accounts. Just none completely fit the bill."

"I'm surprised the son wasn't—"

"Oh, believe me," Winslow exclaimed. "*Everyone* was surprised by that."

The Coopers were an affluent family located in Upstate New

York. At an annual dinner party late the previous year, the entire clan had been murdered. All except one. The crime continued to plague local authorities and even those on the federal level, yet Winslow's carefree attitude told a different story — one worrying to the director.

"Well, I'd be interested in hearing more about your field work. Especially considering you'll be handling various cases for us with the team."

"You mean…?" She paused. "I thought I might not have your approval."

Metcalf stood, hand extended. "Greg worked it all out before."

Winslow joined her, and the pair shared an awkward shake before separating. Their eyes remained locked, sizing up the other. Whatever else Winslow portrayed during their time together, one thing was certain: she was unafraid of Metcalf's disapproval. There wasn't a worry in the world over being asked to leave, like the position was locked thanks to Sullivan. If Metcalf had missed a detail as large as a new recruit, what else was she missing?

Metcalf cleared her throat. Rushing feet greeted her as the door opened. "Why don't we take a walk and get you familiar with the place? If you'd like I can have someone show you around Bethesda as well after we get your living arrangements situated."

"Deputy Director Sullivan already took care of that. I spent the week unpacking. I did some sightseeing to get the lay of the land."

Metcalf led the way from her office, almost stumbling out the door and barely able to contain her anger. Sullivan had broken standard protocol on every level and she was being asked to embrace it. Her distraction caused her to nearly collide into the first figure to round the corner at the same moment.

"Director?" The young blond in the polka-dot skirt recovered from the close call, a distraught look on her face and a pen clutched tight between her fingers. "I didn't see you coming."

"Not a problem, Stephanie." Metcalf brushed her pants while she caught her breath. "Agent Winslow, have you had the chance to meet my assistant, Stephanie Atwater?"

"I have."

"Winslow and I were about to start our tour," Metcalf continued. "What is it?"

Stephanie leaned close with a piercing gaze. "Agent Riley."

"Is he here to meet our new member?" The hour chimed along her wristwatch. For the last few weeks, Ben's typical arrival time had landed somewhere between late and egregiously late. It was another detail yet to be addressed—Metcalf's to-do list grew by the second.

"No," Stephanie said. "He's been escorted to Fort Meade."

"The Council?"

Stephanie nodded. "It appears so."

Winslow inched closer. "Is everything all right?"

Metcalf stopped her with a raised finger and a disarming smirk. The concerned director pulled Stephanie across the hall. Sparse details passed between them in whispers.

Stephanie explained the bus stop incident and the chase that had occurred. What else could be gleaned from Ben's arrival at the headquarters of the NSA was conjecture at best and Stephanie understood to keep such thoughts to a minimum with her boss.

Metcalf nodded, questioning what was available yet never pushing for the impossible. Letting the news sink in, she ran her nails along her chin. Her forced smile returned when she faced the curious newcomer across the corridor.

"I hate to do this, Abigail."

"I understand," Winslow said. "You have to go."

"I do. Yes."

"Maybe Ms. Atwater can show me around?"

Stephanie pointed down the hall. "I'm needed as well."

"Ah."

Metcalf scanned the area for a solution and found one in the form of a scrawny waif of a technician; Support Services was labeled on his lapel. He rushed for the men's room on the other side of their position, halting at the sight of them.

"One moment please," Metcalf called. The man's eyes bulged at the sound of her voice. He pointed to his chest and she offered a nod of confirmation. "Thank you—"

"Jeff."

"I know who you are, Jeff."

"You do?"

Metcalf huffed. "Everyone is a comedian."

"I'm sorry, Director," Jeff said. He nervously shuffled around them. His eyes clearly begged for relief only obtained by the men's room just out of reach. "It's just—"

"Don't make groveling your go-to move, Jeff."

"I—"

"And don't apologize again."

Panic filled Jeff's eyes as he searched for an appropriate response. "Oh, God."

"Jeff," Metcalf said in a calm, soft tone. "Please show our new agent here around. Take her to the Archive and the briefing room. Be sure to stop by our training facilities. I expect a thorough job."

"But, I—" He shifted for the men's room.

"Jeff," Metcalf said with a sigh. "After you go to the bathroom is fine."

"Oh, thank God." He ran into the room and didn't look back.

Metcalf tossed a smile to the waiting recruit. "Wonderful. You're all set."

"Car's waiting," Stephanie beckoned.

The pair moved for the exit, their pace brisk. Metcalf peered back twice. She was still unable to understand Winslow's recruitment. Nor was she able to figure out how to handle Sullivan for recruiting her in the first place.

On top of all that, now there was an off-the-books meeting with one of her agents with the Council? Why would they convene in secret? The details piled up too quickly, all missed despite her diligence and her need to be in control of all aspects of the DSA.

"I want some damn answers. Now."

CHAPTER TEN

In the grand scheme of things there were few places Morgan disliked more than Mt. Sinai Hospital. From the parking nightmare in downtown Baltimore to the reception area—even the personnel serving as gatekeepers to the public—everything in the place was sterile.

Where there should have been life there was nothing more than efficiency for the sake of convenience. Not to say people cared less for the patients. Doctors swore an oath, and the nurses followed up and fulfilled the needs of their patients. No, the apathy was in the air, a thick wave of exhaustion that came from the never-ending fight against death's embrace.

She rushed along hallways. Her badge, a permanent fixture in her hand, answered any pressing questions from concerned staffers. Her mind, her steps, her every thought was locked on the message left on her phone.

HE NEEDS YOU.

Why now? Why, when everything was finally coming together for her? How was it that whenever the future began to brighten, when light showed the way forward, the shadows of the past returned for another visit?

Christmas lights dangled along hallways, multi-colored bulbs guiding her through the ICU. Mistletoe and garland decorated the stairwells and the stations intermixed along the floor. It was an uplifting notion, though it fell flat in the solemn wing.

Few staff members circulated along the hall. No visitors waited along the staggered benches of the wing. She was too early for that crowd, but she refused to wait for permission to find out what had called her to this long-forgotten place.

Baltimore—her hometown. She had been born and raised by a penitent stay-at-home mother and a regretful father with a limiting career and no dreams. They had merely survived, a lesson taught early to their children.

Morgan carried that lesson throughout her entire life.

She stopped halfway down the corridor, her flats squeaking against the freshly mopped tile. The closed door held no secrets thanks to the name plastered at the top of the medical record. The file sat in a small bin beside the room number, taunting her for confirmation.

Glass surrounded the door frame; thick, narrow windows gave a clear view within. No lights beamed from inside. A shadow hovered on the back wall thanks to a series of monitors displaying vitals from the patient. He lay on the bed, eyes shut to the world. For a moment the worst thought imaginable entered her mind, one she'd carried with her the entire snowy drive in from Bethesda. The thought had followed her for years—ever since the last time she saw him in this state.

Then his chest heaved slowly, the folds of the hospital sheets rising with each stolen breath. The shallow beeping of the machines accompanied the effort.

"Dammit," she uttered. She swiped at watery eyes, while she watched his chest rise and fall with his breath.

"Excuse me." A hand grazed her elbow. Morgan flinched back in surprise, her heart skipping a beat against the rhythm of the monitor.

A short man in a white coat stood at her side, though his head only came up to her shoulder. He wore thick glasses. His receding hairline was poorly hidden by a few long strands along the top of his head. The badge attached to his coat offered her a name, Dr. Kevin Miriam.

"Sorry," he said, hand falling to his side. "Visiting hours are later today. Is there something I can help you with?"

Words failed her. Explanations stretched too thin for her unexpected arrival to this place. In response she offered her badge. His eyes raced along to catch the specifics of her identity before she tucked it back in her pocket.

"Okay, Agent," Miriam said, his tongue dragging out each

sound. It was a common tactic used when searching for a calm approach instead of the opening instinct most chose to share when presented with a problem. "I still don't understand—"

"Can you tell me what happened to this patient?" she asked, her voice sharper than she'd intended. Her forceful tone stunned the doctor for a brief interval before he reached for the record waiting beside the door.

He reviewed it briefly. "OxyContin—quite a lot, from the looks of his chart. He had a prescription."

"For years," Morgan muttered.

"He must have been stockpiling. We pumped his stomach of the drug. It was lucky we arrived in time, considering."

"How?" The question came naturally, though it wasn't relevant. How they had been able to arrive so quickly didn't matter as long as the result saved him, yet she required the answer.

The file settled under the doctor's arm. "From what I've been told, his son was the one who found him. Terrible thing for the boy. He and his mother are with one of our counselors downstairs."

Morgan nodded. She hadn't considered the possibility of seeing them when she made the drive to Baltimore. She hoped to avoid any unnecessary conflict during her visit.

"He'll pull through?"

Miriam sighed, resting hard against the heels of his feet. "If he wants to. Medically speaking, he will. We're filtering the rest of the drugs out while keeping him sedated to make him more comfortable. But honestly? I've seen patients like him before. It's a mental battle. We'll offer counselors, programs, whatever we can. Unfortunately, that's the best we can do on our end. The rest is up to him."

She understood completely. The pull to help those in need had driven her to the medical profession; it caused her to commit to the act of saving lives. When the bureaucracy of the domestic field had interfered with her work she moved to the military, serving in multiple war-torn countries.

Every life mattered, but only if it mattered to the person being saved. Some were simply a lost cause from the start, depending on their frame of mind. It was her greatest concern when it came to the man in the room.

"That's what I'm afraid of," she said, her eyes locked on the rise and fall of the man's chest.

"I'm sorry, Agent, but your interest in Mr. Dunleavy is what, exactly?"

She smirked. It always surprised her to hear him spoken in such a way. *Mr. Dunleavy*. To her, he was always Ty, short for Tyrese.

"Personal, Doctor," Morgan answered. "He's my brother."

CHAPTER ELEVEN

Words failed Metcalf upon entering Fort Meade. Her every step was questioned by security stationed at the gate and within the building. Initial responses were swallowed back, the reason behind her arrival unnecessary for anyone other than the Council itself.

By the time she reached the conference room her heart had started pounding in her chest at the thought of what had already transpired—at what could have possibly been at the heart of their questioning of Ben Riley.

His recruitment had been irregular, to say the least. Ben was a beat cop. Compared to dozens of viable options at the federal level, he had minimal experience. She needed that distance, that separation from the norm, for where the DSA was headed. With what she believed to be buried beneath the surface of their organization—and, in truth, hidden from every agency associated with them—Metcalf required an outsider perspective.

Ben fit the bill, for even more than the reasons listed in the back of her mind. She had prepared to argue the point with anyone who believed otherwise. However, to avoid the conflict entirely, Metcalf had made no mention of the decision-making process at all, forcing the Council to accept her choice without a single question asked.

Upon their arrival the receptionist had mentioned a performance evaluation. Had the Council created a new level of scrutiny in response to her independent hiring? Hollis had warned her about following proper procedure with his recent impromptu visit. Could that be the reason why Sullivan disregarded protocol to place Winslow in their midst? More details slipped through the cracks, these of her own making.

She needed to close them up before any real damage was done.

"I'm going to give you one chance to do the right thing here."

Kanigher and Martin, long-standing agents of the NSA, stood transfixed. They barred entry into the conference room.

"Can't help you there," Kanigher said.

"Orders," his colleague clarified.

Metcalf grimaced. "I have a few of my own. The first is to move. Now."

"Not going to happen," Martin said.

"Bobby," Metcalf said to Kanigher, capturing his gaze. "You have to let me in there."

"I can't help you with that, Susan," the agent answered.

"Director." Stephanie's fist clenched at her side. Martin smirked at his partner, though the latter refused to goad her further. Both continued their best impression of a statue in regards to her request. Stephanie stepped forward, readying her own reply to the situation. Metcalf stopped her, hand cradling her elbow. The director shook her head slightly, and her assistant complied.

Before Metcalf returned to the debate at hand, the door creaked open. A single figure escaped the darkness within. Sullivan hurried to close the door, but not before Metcalf managed to catch a glimpse of Stallworth at the head of the table.

"Give us a minute, gentlemen," Sullivan said, slipping between the two guards. They shot obstinate glares, a reminder to the deputy director who they truly served in the pecking order. Sullivan rolled his eyes. "Try to keep the damn things holstered for once."

The deputy led his superior across the hall to a break room. The door closed behind him, leaving their entourage to wait.

The room offered a number of round tables with four metal chairs at each. Two refrigerators sat along the far wall, and there were cabinets and a counter installed between them for storage. A coffee maker and water cooler provided some much-needed refreshments.

Sullivan made no apologies, proffered no regret over the meeting occurring less than fifteen yards away. Metcalf did the same in her silence, instead focusing on a small paper cup of water, which she drained then crushed under her grip.

"Now, Susan—"

"What the hell, Greg?" Metcalf snapped, setting the tone.

Sullivan's hands rose, blocking the verbal beating. "I was going to call."

"But what? Forgot the number?"

"An elderly joke? Really, Susan?"

"Really, Greg?" Metcalf huffed. "An evasion?"

"You were in meetings," Sullivan replied.

"Cut the crap," she shot back. "Was this really a last-minute decision? These people don't make last-minute decisions. They can't even validate starting a conversation without eighteen rounds of voting."

"You forgot to mention the catered meals between votes," Sullivan said.

Metcalf let out a long breath, hands to her hips. "Dammit, Greg. I should be in there."

Sullivan scratched his thin beard, unable to look at her. "They don't want you in there."

"He's my agent."

"Under review by your superiors. We all have bosses we need to keep happy."

"That's what this is?" Metcalf asked in disbelief. "An actual assessment? Outside my purview? This is not how things are done."

"I know, Susan. But things change."

"I recruited Ben," Metcalf said. "I'm his advocate. I should be in the room."

"He'll be fine."

"They should be talking to *me*."

Sullivan shook his head. "They want to talk to Agent Riley. Without a vocal DSA Director in the mix."

"This is about me?"

Sullivan rubbed the back of his neck. "That's not what I said."

"Don't play me, Greg," Metcalf said. "You were in the room with him. Tell me what is going on."

"You want to know?" Sullivan said. "Let me be in the room. Ben will be fine."

None of this made sense to her. From the concept of an evaluation for one on her staff to the way they had brought Ben in.

Instead of escorting him from the office, or even having the meeting at the warehouse, they had surveilled his bus stop. It had been in the works for longer than a spur-of-the-moment meeting.

Which meant Sullivan was lying.

The situation never would have occurred with his predecessor. When Grissom had stood at her side they were a well-oiled machine. Every decision had come from two sides of the department, instead of unilaterally. Jacob Grissom supported the work and trusted in Metcalf to lead the agency. The plans they had made together mattered. Now, thanks to her inability to see every piece on the board, everything threatened to fall apart.

"I'll be here," she muttered.

"Fine," Sullivan said as the corner of his lip upturned at the admission. He reached for the door handle. "Keep the tantrums to a minimum. And Susan? Don't mistake a routine assessment for oversight."

"Hard not to right now."

Sullivan nodded. "I'll keep you updated."

"Do that."

The door closed behind him and she stared after him. The questions hammered against her, though she buried them for the moment. None would help, and none would make this any easier—the waiting game perpetrated by her superiors and subordinates alike.

Metcalf pulled a fresh cup from the stack and filled it. A small swig sated her thirst. Then she crushed the cup. Liquid slipped from the lip and between her fingers to the floor. It reminded her of all the little details she had missed of late. Now, thanks to Sullivan and the Council, they were starting to catch up to her.

CHAPTER TWELVE
Kentucky - 2010

To call the house palatial was an understatement. Lincoln exited his Jeep, eyes never leaving the front of the massive home of the Engers Estate. It sat in the center of an eighteen-acre arena filled with woodlands, a personal three-hole golf course, and an Olympic-sized in-ground pool. Another pool was inside the manor, next to the entertainment room. Or so Lincoln recalled reading in a number of magazines dedicated to the privileged family from Clay County.

A silent, brooding fellow greeted Lincoln as he shut the door to his vehicle. Without a sound, the long shadow wearing a heavy suit despite the early autumn heat led the awestruck Lincoln toward the front of the manor. To the side of the doors were two men. Each wore an earpiece and a shoulder holster.

Secret Service.

Typically reserved for presidents, both current and former, there were exceptions guaranteeing protection for those needing it. Foreign dignitaries and heads of state received the honor. Thanks to an executive order from the White House, so did the Minority Leader of the Senate. Even while gated from the world at the estate, protection was a necessity thanks to threats made against the man.

Lincoln felt out of place among the agents, though he shared their vocation. That morning, instead of his standard suit and earpiece, he found himself wearing a light polo and jeans. He was definitely out of place among the pomp of the manor, as indicated from the stern glower thrown his way by his guide.

The doors opened to the manor and Lincoln was ushered into

the foyer. A spiral staircase on both sides led to a second-floor balcony, which ran the length of the room. A gorgeous brunette leaned on the railing above, watching him closely upon entry to the home. Lincoln cared little for the look. He was more concerned with the devilish smile of Marcus Engers.

"There he is," Marcus pronounced, ditching the model on his arm. The kid—calling him a young man was still a stretch in Lincoln's mind—started down the stairs with arms outstretched for his company. "Glad you could make it, pal."

"I was surprised to hear from you," Lincoln said, allowing the embrace from his former subordinate. The truth was, the surprise came not from hearing from Marcus—he had been calling incessantly since learning of Lincoln's current position. Rather, Lincoln himself was surprised he had answered the phone.

It wasn't a statement on the kid, more on the memories stirred up by the sound of his voice. Nightmares traveled, overseas and across years, plaguing the exhausted ex-soldier. With each message left, with each cry for attention from Marcus, came the screams of Dietrich and Vogel.

"Yeah, I could tell from the stunned silence when you picked up."

Lincoln's head lowered, and he tried to bury the nightmares as well as the memory of the men who served at his side. "I don't do well with phones."

Marcus chuckled, hand clenched tight to Lincoln's shoulder to guide him deeper into the estate. "Yeah, you're more of a person-to-person, face-to-face, kinda guy."

"Something like that."

"Same here, same here," Marcus said. "Come on in already. Don't let the size wow you too much."

"I've seen bigger."

Marcus stopped. After catching the glint of Lincoln's smirk, he shoved the burly man ahead. "Ass."

They continued along a wide corridor into the entertainment room. A fully-stocked bar sat at their right. Plush couches filled the center of the room. Windows took up the far wall from end to end. On the opposite side of the glass was an indoor swimming pool with crystal clear water.

"I am glad you could make it," Marcus said, heading straight for the bar. He twisted the lid from a half-filled bottle of whiskey and poured a splash into the closest glass. When offered a glass the off-duty agent waved it down. Marcus shrugged, closing up the bottle to join his friend in the center of a pair of rarely used couches.

Lincoln sat along the armrest, inquisitive eyes taking in his surroundings. His entire apartment could fit within the foyer. Hell, his apartment complex would only take up a quarter of the estate. Both men had bled for their country, paid the price in their service. Only one of them, however, possessed the coin to cover the tab.

"Turns out I had the week off."

The smile grew on the kid's face. "I might have made a call about that."

"Marcus."

"Don't give me that scowl, Lincoln." He waved down the glare. "Hide the grumpiness and try to relax for a minute."

Lincoln took a sharp breath. His need for work was difficult to explain to outsiders. Earning his stripes with the Secret Service after three tours meant more to him than he cared to admit. The work, however, while grating at times, was a pure service to the country. To have someone make a call and remove him from duty for a simple meeting went against every bone in his body.

"I wanted to run something by you. A job I think you might be perfect for."

"I have a—"

"I know your work is important to you," the kid interrupted. "One lousy day of fun won't kill you."

"Plus a job offer, it seems."

"Yes," Marcus exclaimed, thankful to be back on track. "I'm very proud of your position, but you could be doing so much more."

"For you?"

"Yes. Well, no. Not just me." Marcus stopped, placing the drink on the coffee table. "For the group that has approached me. Lincoln, the people involved? They're going to change the way we view the world."

"Not overly dramatic at all."

Marcus laughed. "You're going to like this. I'm talking about saving lives on the front lines of conflicts around the world. That's only one aspect of the group."

"What group, Marcus? What have you been up to since you've been back?" Specifics had been vague on the phone and in every email shared between the two. Most of the information shared by Marcus had been about life on the estate. Marcus' dating profile held more details than he'd shared on a personal level with his old unit commander.

"They call themselves—"

"Is this the young man you told me about, Marcus?"

Both turned toward the new voice in the room. A man of fifty stood proudly on the landing. He wore khakis and a dark polo. His salt-and-pepper hair pressed tightly against his scalp. It was perfect, just like his grin: the feature that put him on the cover of more magazines than any other politician short of the president. Senator Morrison Engers was larger than life and wouldn't have it any other way.

"It is," Marcus said as the joy quickly faded from his face. "Lincoln, I'd like to—"

Morrison stepped around his son, hand extended. "I've heard quite a bit about you, Sergeant MacKenzie."

"It's an honor, sir." Lincoln shook hands with the man. It took every ounce of resistance to keep from saluting.

"I like him," Morrison said as he pulled away. He walked over to the bar and filled a small glass with orange juice from a carafe at the end of the oak counter.

"Your work on the Committee on Armed Services has saved a lot of lives overseas, sir. It truly is an honor."

"I appreciate it," the senator toasted before sipping his drink. "And it's Morrison."

"Lincoln."

"An agent, my son tells me. Secret Service is quite a privilege."

"Yes, well, I try to earn it every day," Lincoln replied. "Your son, however, seemed to have some thoughts on my career choice."

Marcus paled at the mention. "Now, Lincoln..."

"I'm sure he did," Morrison interjected. "He has many thoughts about other people's choices. All he needs is some time to sort out his own. After the conference this weekend, that is."

"Of course," Marcus said. "But Dad, if I could—"

"Don't *dad* me," his father answered in a stern tone. "I'm sure

Lincoln would agree a man should stand on his own. He should find his own strength and make his own opportunities."

"I don't think it's my place to say, sir."

"Morrison," the senator corrected.

"Right."

Marcus finished his drink and stood. "Thanks, Dad." He smiled at his former commanding officer and patted his shoulder. "Seriously, Lincoln. You should hear him shower praise on me when the donors are around. Never fails to maintain a strong family image when it counts, right, Dad?"

"Strength coming from you, Marcus? Maybe a full tour of duty would have instilled that in you, Son."

Crestfallen, Marcus fell back on his heels and away from the two intimidating forces in the room. "I would love to recount more heartwarming tales of togetherness, but I have a conference to oversee." Marcus turned to his father. "Remember that Mr. Weingard would like a word tonight about—"

"I remember," Morrison said. "Thank you."

"Yes, sir," Marcus intoned. "Now if I could steal Lincoln for—"

"Actually, I would like to speak to our guest, if that's all right with you?"

"I don't—"

Morrison's grin cut through his son. "I won't steal him for long."

Marcus nodded in defeat. He reached out to the guest caught in the middle of the affair, who wished nothing more than to be anywhere else, and shook his hand.

"Lincoln."

Marcus turned to depart, Lincoln calling after him to no avail. "Marcus?"

The young man had barely reached the end of the room before Morrison pulled Lincoln back to their pending conversation. His voice softened, yet the volume was enough to catch his son's ears before he was out of range.

"No ambition. Or maybe there's too much and not enough drive to achieve. It's a problem quite prevalent in our country these days."

Lincoln stood as Morrison found a comfortable position near the windows overlooking the pool. "What can I do for you, sir?"

"As I said before, I've heard quite a bit about you. You did save my son's life, after all."

Images of Dietrich and Vogel flashed, though the nightmares were quickly suppressed. "There were others—"

Morrison nodded. "You saved him, Lincoln. Your *leadership* saved him. Your drive. You did it. I never had the chance to thank you."

"I would never ask for thanks."

"I realize that as well. You weren't easy to track down after you landed state-side."

Lincoln nodded. He hadn't been accessible for almost a year after returning from his last tour. He'd tried to track down his brother. When he had finally managed to find his older sibling it was too late. Dante had been killed in a drive-by shooting. A drug deal had gone wrong and he had been caught in the middle of it. Lincoln knew Dante's role in the situation, one he'd played for over a decade after he dropped out of school—and out of Lincoln's life. Still, he was family and family deserved a proper goodbye.

Afterward, Lincoln drifted. He carried out odd jobs, nothing that required him to plant too many roots. Just enough to live. When he had run into Captain Thomas of all people, his former S.O. had provided the kick in the ass Lincoln needed to return to the world. A kick, and the opportunity to serve a purpose again.

"I was figuring things out."

"Understandable," Morrison admitted. "It changes you. War. Conflict of any kind, really. It focuses you until you want to be lost for a while. To be someone else. I did get lucky enough to learn about your current assignment."

"It's—"

"No need to sugarcoat it," the senator continued. "Transport runs are not exactly the mean streets of Sangin, right? Anyway, I made a few calls."

"Sir, I wish you wouldn't have." The truth was, the man was right. Pompous ambassadors needed protecting the same as everyone else. Airport pick-ups and drop-offs, however, left the ex-soldier feeling restless and unfulfilled.

Morrison shook his head. "Just asking you to hear me out. If it doesn't work for you, I'll leave you to my son's latest and greatest scheme to soak in more of the limelight. Might be a nice change of pace for you, but not really what men like us are built for."

Lincoln smirked at the admission and the senator caught his look. They shared a laugh. "Yes," Morrison said, "I do include myself in that category despite my position. We serve something greater than ourselves, don't we?"

He didn't need a response to know Lincoln's answer. He had fought to find the right cause, to make a real difference, ever since he lost his mother.

"The truth of the matter is there have been threats against me and my family. I consider them overblown. The president, however, does not and I serve at the man's pleasure even if our ideologies run on different sides of the aisle. I need someone I can trust to lead my protective detail. I want that to be you."

"Me?"

"What do you say?"

"I suppose I'm the one who owes you thanks now, sir."

"Morrison."

Lincoln shook his head. "Sir."

Morrison grinned and took the man's hand. "Very well then. Welcome aboard, Agent MacKenzie."

CHAPTER THIRTEEN

"I won't sit," the wavering agent muttered, though he did lower his pistol.

"You don't have to, Agent," the Witness said as a smirk spread across his lips. He eased deeper into the chair, as relaxed as ever, seemingly knowing the outcome long before Lincoln had ever come to the conclusion. "I can see it in your eyes. You want what I am offering: answers. You need them."

He did. Ever since Bellbrook Lincoln had sought out a reason behind his tenure at the DSA. An overarching purpose to explain the sacrifices necessary to keep going, to stand tall and find the strength his mother believed inherent in him.

"And you supposedly have them?"

The Witness nodded. "Think of it. Think of having a true purpose again, away from faceless organizations and government bureaucracy. No more hidden agendas. You could do true good for this country and the world, as you promised your mother so long ago."

"True good?" Lincoln scoffed. "The slaughter of every man, woman, and child in Bellbrook sounds more like the work of a murderer than a hero."

"You're wrong."

"You killed those people."

"I saved them!" the Witness shouted, the reaction startling to Lincoln. A chink in his casual calm that drove him back a step. "Your interference brought the DOD into play. *They* killed those people, Lincoln. Not me. I saved them just as I hope to save everyone."

"How?"

"Their change was merely the beginning, though it didn't reach fulfillment."

"No."

The Witness leaned forward. "Others attempt to stymie my work, Lincoln. And why? Do you know?"

Ruth was alive? As a tree? Like a chrysalis for a caterpillar forcing a transformation to some next stage? It was an impossibility to the grounded soldier. People were alive or they were dead. There was no in-between, yet the Witness protested louder and stronger with each allegation.

Proclaiming his innocence was not a strange tactic. Most did when confronted with their crimes. However, his words hammered at Lincoln as the truth.

"No."

"Of course you don't," the Witness chided. "You're not important enough to them—not vital enough to their plans. You're just the brute, the soldier. Take an order. Fulfill it. Stick to strict objectives. Do not deviate. All the while you have no clue as to what your own people are planning."

Wheels within wheels. He spoke about the agendas and ambitions of people instead of the ideals of a nation. Lincoln fought for the betterment of people, pushed to make a life for himself in that work. Whenever he failed, when someone—not him, never him—fell at his side, the sacrifice made him question such deeds.

Was it worth it? Did any of it matter anymore? Not according to the Witness, who held the secrets behind his shattering shell of an existence.

"Enlighten me," the weary agent said.

"I have seen things, Lincoln," the Witness began. "The future. For all of us. We stand at a tipping point. Falter and everything slides away from us. The DSA threatens everything."

"Not possible. The DSA is a small department within the government. We hardly make a dent in the caseload we have."

"Yet each one is vital, each one a piece of a larger puzzle that has been growing ever since the DSA's inception."

"How?"

"Did your director explain the origins of the Department of Special Assignments? Or, as it was once called, the Department of Scientific Anomalies?"

"It wasn't a department at all," Lincoln recounted. "Men and women from other agencies investigated the unknown on their own time. They attempted to explain the inexplicable."

"They sought to understand technology and science that had stretched the boundaries of the natural world."

"Like Bellbrook."

"Like *everything*, Lincoln. Genetic re-sequencing, recombinant DNA manipulation, the Apollo missions, and more. In four millennia we barely scratched the surface of our potential as a species, yet in the last century we have leaped farther and imagined greater than our brightest thinkers thought possible. Have you ever questioned why that is?"

"That's what the DSA has been looking for?"

"Right from the start. Without success."

"Until now. Metcalf wouldn't—"

The Witness shook his head. "Not all within your precious organization are aware of what is happening in the background. They are oblivious to the growing threat circling your cases. Only a few, working in secret, manipulate your purpose for their own, just as they work to undermine my efforts in bringing them to light. I am trying to stop them from waking the disaster to come."

"Impossible," Lincoln replied. "You're saying these people are abusing science and technology for their own ends? Manipulating us, the DSA, into helping their agenda? There's no way. We would know. Someone would find out the truth. You can't hide something like that."

The Witness laughed. "They've done it for decades."

"Who?"

"A powerful group with more money and resources than most small nations. Yet they remain ignorant to the true threat approaching, thanks to their manipulations. Blinded by greed, they would offer up the world of tomorrow for the profit of today."

"Give me names. Dates. Something concrete," Lincoln demanded.

The Witness clasped his hands together, fingers interlaced tight in front of his covered eyes. "The Wellspring."

"What is the—?"

The ominous figure stopped him, shaking his hand at the query. "There are three events. Three pivotal moments they seek to control. The Wellspring is the first and has been theirs for some time now. But something has changed, and events are moving faster than before. If we lose the Wellspring, if the signal reaches terminal point, it will begin."

"What?"

"A greater fall than you can possibly imagine. For everyone."

"How?" Lincoln asked, incredulous. "How can you know any of this?"

The Witness tapped the frame of his spectacles. "I know this because I have seen it. In truth, I would give everything to forget that I have."

"The DSA is evil and you're the Lone Ranger riding to the rescue?" Lincoln said with a huff, rubbing at his eyes. "You can see why I have trouble swallowing this."

"I can."

"Then why? Why bring me here to tell me this?"

"Because of the next choice you make."

Lincoln paused. Just when it seemed his confusion had reached a peak, the man sitting before him found a way to push the limit. "What?"

The Witness raised his wrist and his watch chirped upon his pale skin. "The ticking clock I mentioned previously. It comes in the form of two armed men in the corridor. They've come to kill me. Let them, and all my answers are lost. If that happens, I can only hope you see the truth soon enough to make a difference. Or, you can save me and get the answers you seek — beginning with the name of the man who killed Morrison Engers."

The Witness was asking Lincoln to save his life while leveraging the unsolved murder of a man who had almost stood as the next President of the United States. Lincoln swallowed his disgust and swiftly moved for the door.

He listened intently for as long as he could, questioning everything. Every word spoken by the man, every assertion against the work Lincoln had been doing for the last four years at the DSA, and even his own wavering resolution to complete the mission at hand and return home. Nothing was certain, yet the Witness seemed to take everything as fact.

Including that two armed men were heading their way.

Lincoln edged the suite door open. He removed the mirror from his vest, and then positioned it low and just outside the thick frame. The cameras were back up and running, the red light reflecting in the glass for a moment as he positioned the mirror to view the hall in full.

Two men approached. They wore suit jackets and shoulder holsters. Neither scanned the hall, and neither bothered checking the angles or seemed to be worried about the cameras. They remained locked on their objective: Room 11-10 and the man within.

Dammit. Lincoln retracted the mirror and closed the door without a sound.

Rounding the corner for the living area, Lincoln paced the length of the room. His time was running out.

The Witness smirked. "I would choose quickly."

CHAPTER FOURTEEN

The clock inched along. The second hand ticked loudly, the sound pounding like a hammer against her skull. Minutes slipped past the hour. There had still been no word. No movement came within the room. No sense of recovery from Tyrese, who continued to rest as the drugs were cycled out of his system. He spent years in recovery and now a relapse?

Morgan's head settled against the glass of the door, lost in memories. No matter the distance, no matter the sacrifice made to bury her mistakes, they always found a way to claw their way to the surface. She wanted to rush into the room, to shake him back to consciousness and demand an answer, even though she knew it would mean nothing.

Miriam finished his rounds and circled back down the corridor. He carried a small cup of water, which he passed along to the weary agent. His questioning attitude faded behind the wall of compassion instilled from a lifetime of service. It was either that or go cold and detached, which was the path she had taken.

A silent word of thanks and a satisfying sip brought a momentary glimmer of kindness to her face. Miriam joined her outside her brother's room.

She sighed after she had emptied the drink. "I'd like to see him. Talk to him when he wakes."

Dr. Miriam fixed his glasses to the bridge of his nose. "That won't be for awhile yet, I'm afraid. Mr. Dunleavy—that is to say, your brother—is heavily sedated right now. We need to assess the damage once the drugs are out of his system—both physically and cognitively."

"So there is some indication of damage?"

"No," Miriam replied, his voice firm yet comforting. "Thanks to the rapid response to his condition I believe he should make a full recovery. However—"

She stopped him with a wave and a nod, accepting the analysis for what it was. "Got it. Think happy thoughts."

His eyes fell. Offering hope was part of the job; she knew that better than most of the unfortunates visiting the ward this day. What it failed to do for them, however, was inform them of the odds of recovery or the rehabilitation to come in response to their injuries. Not enough information was readily available for Tyrese, nor would it be for some time, especially if this was not the end of the story. There was always the chance he might make another attempt, be it with OxyContin again or something more definitive.

Hope was all the doctor had to give, and she took it graciously.

"I'll update you as soon as I can," Miriam said. "Same with the immediate family."

He left her to her silence, yet that was only on the surface. Her thoughts screamed, echoing between her ears. She had nearly forgotten about Tyrese's family. In the hour lost to her regrets and guilt over the situation in the ICU she had failed to realize the passing time also brought about the start of visiting hours to the ward.

Folks trickled in from the entrance at the far end of the corridor. They passed nurses attending to various needs. They were greeted with kindness and warmth from those kept for observation. Their laughter outweighed their pain.

Morgan felt none of it. All she experienced was the cold of the winter outside, rushing along the hall with each entrant. Each new visitor brought a sickening agony in the pit of her stomach. She hadn't come for a fight, hadn't made the trek from Bethesda to argue. Not with her brother and definitely not with his wife.

Checking her watch, Morgan decided to step away from her brother's room. Ty would sleep for some time, and a break would afford her a chance to think about what she would say after so much time apart. It would also save her the trouble of answering those questions from others.

Unfortunately, her plan arrived too late to act. A pair of visitors entered the wing, though they were slow to approach. The mother ambled in, holding back the well of terror behind her eyes. She displayed strength where there was only sadness. It was a front necessary for her companion—her son of nine.

He's so big. How did he get so damn big?

Jamal stopped at the sight of her. "Aunt Morgan?"

Morgan smiled, bending low with arms spread. "Come here, buddy."

His mother struggled to keep him in place, and she finally lost hold as he ran to greet an aunt not seen in years. Morgan squeezed him tight, eyes closed. Her entire soul ached for this—his innocence and his warmth. It had been far too long.

"What are you doing here?" Jamal asked, stepping back. "Dad said you left."

"I know," Morgan said. "I did leave, but I came back. Now bring it back in here, mister. I need another hug."

She held him close, refusing to allow the moment to slip by. Struggling against her affection, the boy ended the hug, but not before her hand grazed his cheek. Tired eyes captured every detail of the nephew she hadn't seen in years. He was lean and muscular, an active child in a world of couch potatoes. He had his father's eyes, striking and sharp, and short-cropped hair. Well on his way to becoming a man.

"What have I said about growing so much?"

Jamal rolled his eyes. "To stop it."

"You never listen." They laughed, lost to the memory of a shared joke. Jamal fell silent for a moment. His father's shadow in the room caught his eye and the boy shuffled for the glass. Morgan joined him. "I heard what happened. Are you okay?"

"He's fine," his mother answered. She pulled him away from the door. Her hands guided him back to the corridor. "Give us a minute, baby. Sit over on the bench and then we'll go see Daddy."

Jamal paused, eyes locked on the room then on his aunt. "But I wanted to talk to Aunt Morgan too."

"Later, buddy," Morgan said. "I promise."

Jamal nodded, starting for the bench. His shoulders slumped; the weight of the day clearly bore down on him once more. His mother failed to notice, anger raging through her body.

Charlotte. It was always an effort to think of her by her actual name and look past the titles that defined her: mother, wife, and breadwinner. Once upon a time, however, Charlotte Powell had been Morgan's best friend. The two of them had taken on the world together, dreaming big no matter who stood in their way.

Now, Morgan stood in her way.

"Your promises don't mean much here."

"Don't, Charlotte."

"What happened to staying the hell away from us?" Charlotte said, the air snapping with each word. It was the same tone Morgan recalled from every conversation shared over the last three years. It was Charlotte's way, and Morgan simply took it in stride.

"I did," Morgan said, her voice little more than a whisper against the growing crowd in the corridor. "I have been. But I thought—"

"You should go."

"No," Morgan said. She took a sharp breath and let it out. "Dammit, just talk to me. You said he was getting better."

After the last bout, after her exile from the family, Morgan had continued to reach out. Never in person—rarely even a phone call, their instinct to argue always present. Mostly through text or email could she keep tabs on the family she lost when she returned from war.

"He was," Charlotte said. The strong, confident posture faded as the young mother leaned along the windows of the room. Her husband was inside, mere feet away, yet it may as well have been miles. "And then he wasn't. The holidays—"

"Are no excuse," Morgan said, a bit too harshly. She regretted the words as soon as they had slipped from her lips.

"To you," Charlotte said. "You were the strong one. And you made sure to mention it every chance you could."

"All I wanted was to help him. To support him."

Charlotte shook her head. "You were nothing but a reminder, Morgan. Don't you see that? Same goes with the damn holidays. With everything."

Morgan's brow furrowed, confused at the lost stare of the woman and the softness of her tone. Charlotte picked at the sleeve of her blouse and pulled it over her wrist. A thick bracelet was latched on, an obstacle to her goal. Morgan reached out, attempting to assist in her struggle. A colorful blotch beneath screamed for her attention.

"Don't—"

Morgan refused to listen, instead lifting the sleeve to view the bruises along the woman's arm. Purple and blue marred once unblemished skin. The former physician tracked the injuries, noticing the way Charlotte's hair fell along her neck. Morgan pushed the strands aside and saw more.

"How long has he been doing this, Charlotte?" she asked, afraid of the answer. "You should have told me!"

Charlotte took a step back, using her jacket to cover her arm. "Get out of here, Morgan. We'll take care of him."

"I can help."

"No," Charlotte said. "You can't. You can't help us. All you do is bring us pain. You're smart enough to understand that, aren't you?"

She turned, a hand extended toward the nearby bench where Jamal sat. How much he'd overheard was not in question, only the amount he would carry with him in the days ahead. Slow to leave the comfort of the seat, the boy of nine returned to his mother's side and slipped his hand in hers.

"Charlotte, please..."

Charlotte stopped at the door, refusing to look at her former friend. "Just leave, Morgan. That's what you're good at."

The door closed behind them. They shut her out of their lives, just as soundly as they had before. She had failed to be there, failed to help when they needed it, and now her efforts fell short.

Charlotte was right. Morgan was best at being away. Morgan had offered them nothing but a constant reminder. She turned for the exit, the day lost to grief. A call to the hospital later would suffice. She didn't need more arguments with her brother or his wife. Nor did she feel it necessary to inflict more pain on her nephew.

A new arrival stopped her at the far end of the hall. He carried a brown paper bag and a steaming beverage. "I brought coffee and a shoulder," Zac called. "Thought you might need both."

CHAPTER FIFTEEN

Ben sat through the inquiry for hours. A steady flow of questions shot his way from across the room. Stallworth and Sullivan handled the heavy lifting. Each query, each insight into his day-to-day activities since joining the DSA, arrived from one of the two.

The others played a more passive role in the affair. They read reports and briefings as well as logs recorded by members of the DSA—from operational support to analysts working in the hub. Each offered their impression of the recent recruit.

Each member of the impromptu assemblage kept their heads down as they read. They placed no emphasis on the language used. They merely dictated reports word for word. They gave no opinion to the information in each report; there was no real value added by their presence.

A fruit smoothie definitely would have helped jazz up the assessment. Ben's eyes struggled to remain focused. The tapping of his foot to the beat of *Tonight, Tonight* barely kept him awake.

Part of the problem lay in a lack of direction on their end. Instead of a clear starting point at his recruitment, they returned to his time in Buffalo, where the questions ranged from his days at the academy to his home life. When the line of inquiry skirted close to his arrest and subsequent conviction, he offered them nothing but silence in response.

"Let's move on from that for the moment," Stallworth or Sullivan would respond, often in tandem, as if they were reading from the same script.

Minimal answers were Ben's way of bucking the system. One-word responses aggravated the main proponents against him, driving them to follow up time and time again without much in the way of information.

What was this about? None of it made sense. They claimed to be performing an assessment of his field work with the DSA, yet they wanted to know about his time in Buffalo? Multiple questions wondered if he had had encounters with the department or any of its personnel before becoming aware of its existence?

The inquiry shifted, eventually, to the last two months and his current position. Unfortunately, each occurrence shuffled the time forward, and the day was lost to queries without purpose or design.

"Getting back to the Bellbrook incident," Sullivan said, his tone never changing, his attitude never tiring. "Mr. Modine attempted to follow procedure and bring the operation to the proper agency, yet he was overruled by Director Metcalf. Is that a true statement?"

There wasn't time for the argument. People were missing, and the DSA had been in a position to do something about it. Ben recalled the discussion from his first day, the tension in the briefing room over the case dropped in their laps from an unknown party.

His response, however, offered little insight into the situation. "Yes. That's correct."

They cared not for the lengthy reply. They cared only for facts, truths without context to make a snap judgment. But how it related to Ben evaded the weary agent. He simply kept up appearances, doing his best to follow along against the random pattern of questions flowing freely from Stallworth and Sullivan.

No conversation was had about the situations at hand. About what he had seen in Bellbrook, about the people they'd found within the small town. No mention at all was made of the Department of Defense's presence and their extreme reaction to the forest of trapped souls.

Instead, they tested his memory on protocol—on the orders given and how they were accomplished or dismissed out of hand. They sought blame for misguided attempts to assist, and Bellbrook started their hunt.

Focus came with each subsequent case. The questions, once random, started to form a pattern. The beating of his foot subsided, his eyes sparked awake, and Ben finished his glass of water. He leaned into each question, asking for a repeat here and there to give him more time to fit them into the growing puzzle laid out by the two inquisitors.

"It was at that moment in Chicago you made the unilateral decision to cut out the FBI, was it not?"

A distortion of the truth, yet Ben rolled with it. The interaction with the man thought to be Connor Hendricks replayed in his mind. Hendricks had deceived them, steered their investigation toward only one possible outcome, one that had failed to sit right with the agent.

"I merely hit the brakes on our partnership to offer a fresh perspective."

Sullivan nodded, never actually hearing the answer. He appeared too interested in the next question, advancing the assessment.

"Was there coordination from Bethesda? Director Metcalf was in the loop for these choices, correct?"

The simple answer was no. Sullivan recognized the fact immediately. When they had gone their own way, leaving Hendricks and what they believed to be the FBI to their own investigation, they had also failed to update the home office.

At first there had been no need — a quick reprieve to look into different options was not outside the standard operating of a covert agency like the DSA. Two separate tracks of thought, two lines of questioning, opened up new avenues of investigating the situation.

Then Zac was abducted. After that, their sole purpose turned to saving one of their own. In the process of saving Zac they learned about Hendricks' duplicity. Unfortunately, they failed to learn the man's true identity before the end.

Or the agenda he served.

None of that mattered to Sullivan, who eyed the stalling agent suspiciously. Stallworth's hands clasped tight before him, crushing the world with his thick sausage-like extensions.

They cared not for Ben's dismissal of Hendricks, the follow up question making that incredibly obvious. They cared not for the secrets held in Bellbrook or the cover-up by the DOD. They focused on a single line of questioning, one it had taken hours to pull apart from the history lesson surrounding Ben.

This wasn't an assessment at all. This was a test.

None of it was about Ben or about the things he had seen during his brief tenure. It was not about the questions sparked from his investigations, or where they might be leading. This was about someone else entirely. A show, perpetrated by the two men, and all centered around the leadership of the DSA.

This was all about Susan Metcalf.

CHAPTER SIXTEEN
Des Moines - 2015

The trip had come at the last minute. Preparation for the senator's arrival had been minimal at best, the advance team given barely an hour before touchdown thanks to the late notice and the even later approval by the lead on the detail. Lincoln continued to debate his decision as he coordinated with local police on how to give the senator a clear exit from the bustling terminal to his car waiting by the service entrance.

That didn't stop Morrison Engers from working the crowd. He saw it as his obligation at this point to shake as many hands as possible no matter the destination. It was a statement to the country and a joy for the man, who grew more and more outgoing in his endeavors. Every event, every occasion was an opportunity for future votes he told Lincoln, while his protective detail kept him moving through the various throngs waiting for the Minority Leader of the Senate of the United States.

Des Moines was not filled with groups of people. A few stragglers, surprised to see the senator being escorted by a tightly packed group of staffers, had stopped for a quick photo. It was not the usual lines that paraded press conferences or charity events, but it was still enough to worry Lincoln.

Morrison shook hands quickly before the pair led their group through the terminal at a brisk pace. "Could that flight have been any longer? *Four* delays? We'll pack the RV next time, right Lincoln?"

Lincoln hesitated. He scanned people as they came into view in the terminal. From the corner of his eye he caught the senator's questioning look. "Yes... Sounds good, sir."

"Lincoln?" Morrison asked. "Don't hold back on me now. Over five years in, I can hear it in your damn steps."

Lincoln understood the sentiment. Time had tightened their bond. The senator was more than a body to protect; he was a friend. Sometimes, however, that became an issue, and he chose distance rather than conversation to remain objective to the task at hand. Unfortunately, conversation always seemed to work better for Morrison.

"Just concerned, sir."

"Those threats are overblown," Morrison said without looking over at Lincoln. He was smiling at a large family who appeared to be waiting for someone.

Lincoln huffed, watching the group carefully as they passed. It was the same reaction the senator had offered for the last five years. Lincoln disagreed with his assessment of the situation. The latest threats in question were the most consistent since the executive order for Secret Service protection had been issued for the senator. Emails. Letters. Voicemails. All had been untraceable, and all spelled an early demise for the senator.

"The Service doesn't think they are, sir."

Morrison waved them off the same way he had when they started. "They don't know political bullying, then."

"I'm not sure this trip is in your best interest right now. Not until we lock down the person or persons responsible."

"This is an opportunity, Lincoln. We were going to announce soon anyway." Morrison slipped his arm over Lincoln's shoulder and pulled him closer. "But if you feel that strongly against our trip you can tell it to our host."

The senator stopped near the service entrance to the terminal. The agent at his side slowly recognized the man waiting for them. He had grown—more muscular, less gangly, yet still one hundred percent Marcus Engers.

"Dad," Marcus said. He shook the man's hand forcefully. Lincoln was unnerved by his look, by the very sound of the man he had once saved in Afghanistan. Fire sat in his eyes, an intensity that hadn't been present previously.

"Marcus. I was surprised to hear you were in Des Moines."

"Opportunity knocked." Marcus reached beyond his father. "Lincoln."

"Marcus." Lincoln shook his hand. Three quick pumps confirmed the added strength of the young man. Lincoln let go of the hand, confused and concerned with the pure joy in Marcus' face. "It's been a while."

"It has," Marcus sneered. "I've been working on a few things."

Morrison moved between them. "My boy and his secrets."

Marcus nodded, tilting his head for the service entrance. Lincoln led the way. He opened the door to inspect the space between them and the limo waiting at the curb. Officers had cordoned the entryway upon their arrival. With the area secure, Lincoln ushered the group into the sunshine.

"Why Des Moines, Marcus?" Lincoln asked.

"Dad loves the Savery, pal." Marcus tilted his head to his father, who nodded. "Won a charity golf tourney a mile or two from here, what was it, twenty years ago?"

Morrison's eyes trailed off in remembrance. "I haven't been able to get back in ages."

"I made sure your suite was available." Marcus put his arm around his father, guiding him to the waiting limousine.

"Is that photo still up?" Morrison said in surprise. Lincoln fell back from them, letting them have their moment. They had never been close, but there were still memories that connected them as a family.

"Of course."

Morrison grinned, reaching for the door of the limo. Marcus rushed in front of him to open it for him. "Thank you, Son."

"My pleasure, Dad."

Morrison slid in the limo, followed by his staffers. Lincoln waited patiently for them to filter inside before moving in front of Marcus.

"I'll need to check the suite. My team will want access to the ballroom for the event as soon as possible, and we'll also need to see any changes made to the guest list. If there is private security involved I'll need contact information to coordinate."

"You sure know how to live it up, don't you?" Marcus grinned from ear to ear. "You'll have it, Lincoln."

Lincoln nodded, slipping into the limo. Before he could pull the door shut, though, Marcus poked his head inside.

"Dad, Reginald Kane was hoping for a few minutes tonight before the big announcement."

"He's coming?" Morrison shifted uncomfortably in his seat. Joy spread across his son's face in response.

"Said he wouldn't miss it." Marcus tapped lightly on the frame of the door. "Now, I have caterers to yell at, so you're on your own until tonight. Oh, and try to smile a little, Lincoln."

The door closed with finality. Lincoln waited a second, listening to the agent in the passenger seat for his status update before the car shifted into traffic. Once they were underway, Lincoln let his gaze drift to the window and the sun overhead. The staffers in the limousine started to work on the day's agenda. Others burrowed into the guest list for the event, figuring out which potential donors were worth face time with the senator, and which could be pushed off for a photo op later in the night. Each paved their careers one dinner at a time.

The senator nodded when necessary, all the while making calls to keep track of things at the home office. Lincoln did his best to ignore the details and focused instead on the light traffic.

His heart fell when they entered downtown proper. The area was cut in two by the Des Moines River, and he turned away as the limo crept up to a large extension bridge guiding them across.

Morrison put his hand to the receiver of the phone, his eyes concerned for the man beside him. "Something on your mind?"

"Hmm?"

"What is it, Lincoln?"

Lincoln shook his head, then took a long moment to shift back to the window and the bridge beneath them. Short shallow breaths made it easier to stomach, one tactic in his arsenal from a lifetime of fear. "Just the bridge, sir. I don't like bridges."

Morrison nodded. He finished the call, then tossed the phone back to one of the staffers. He settled along his seat. "Still nervous about Marcus' plans?"

"More than ever," Lincoln replied. The last-minute notice and the lack of preparation unnerved the seasoned agent. He'd known better than to approve the trip, yet had relented to Morrison as he always did despite his concern for the man's safety.

"He tries too hard and at the wrong things. Someday he'll figure it out. But he's family." Morrison sighed and sank deeper into the custom leather. "I can't wait for a shower and the minibar."

Lincoln nodded, his heart slowing with the bridge fading behind them. The Savery came into view — still blocks away, yet its shadow loomed toward them. "I'll have the room swept immediately. I really do wish we'd had more time upfront with this to prepare."

Morrison patted Lincoln's shoulder, smiling at the man he called friend more often than employee. "You worry too much, Lincoln. I've been here a dozen times in the past. Besides the occasional bout of overindulgence, nothing ever happens in Des Moines. Ever."

CHAPTER SEVENTEEN

There weren't enough angles. Preparation was a critical factor of any operation: knowing the lay of the land as if imprinted on the back of your eyelids before stepping foot in the room. The living space offered no defensible position. The bathroom was a dead end. The glass shower door provided more hazard than cover. Lincoln had all the knowledge necessary, but not enough angles to make it work in his favor.

And definitely not enough time.

Two men approached, their footfalls beating in tune with his heart. Lincoln could only be sure of the pistols strapped to their shoulder holsters. Whatever else hid under their jackets, their intentions were clear—though not who they were or what organization they represented. Telling the good from the bad was becoming a cruel joke of a game. The Witness kept things light from his permanent post in his chair.

"I imagine they appear quite eager, don't they?" he asked with a wry grin. "Did you see the blood lust in their eyes, Lincoln?"

The frustrated agent's scowl blasted the unfazed target.

"Similar to your own, I would imagine," the Witness said.

Was this the right move? The Witness remained the known commodity of the equation. Because of his actions, the town of Bellbrook had been wiped from the map. There was no question his work had resulted in the deaths of thousands. It was merely semantics when assigning the blame.

He claimed innocence. Hell, he also claimed knowledge of every perpetrator in Lincoln's life. From the man who assassinated Senator Morrison Engers in this very same hotel suite to the true villains behind Ruth Heller's loss.

Answers. That was what the man sold to Lincoln, and he ate it up. Not without reservations, of course. There would always be doubt when looking at the man and his smug smile. Something about not being able to view his eyes rubbed Lincoln the wrong way; there was a distrust that carried over to his explanation of events.

Now, however, Lincoln was forced to decide. Accept the validity of the man's so-called answers, or allow them to be lost at the hands of the two men outside in the hall.

"These decisions must weigh on you," the Witness said. "Who to save and who to kill?"

"Shut up," Lincoln spat. "Who are they?"

The Witness wagged his finger. "Tick tock, Agent. It's time to make a decision. Will it be my death to satisfy your need for revenge, or will it be my answers so you can find your true purpose again?"

"Damn you. If this is some trick, I'll—"

"Kill me?" the Witness chuckled. "Oh, dear me. Whatever will I do?"

"Just keep quiet."

Lincoln scrambled for the bedroom, the last refuge in the suddenly cramped suite. A dresser positioned next to the door provided a small corner of darkness, so he tucked close to the shadowed wall. His breath caught in his lungs, and lips clamped shut as the suite door opened and steps approached cautiously.

"Gentlemen," the Witness said, his voice carrying easily into the next room. "So glad you could make it. I would offer you some breakfast, but I'm afraid I've spoiled the meal with my clumsiness."

Both were tall and muscular under loose-fitting pants and jackets. When they entered the living space, they separated. One maintained a position near the entrance, an eye toward the bathroom on the left.

His companion circled the room in a wide arc. The Witness never reacted, grinning at his new company. The second man rounded the chairs and the dining table for the window. He pulled the thick curtains open, allowing light to shower in from the outside. Content at the lack of shadows in the space, the figure held firm behind their objective.

The first left his position as his colleague covered the room. He took the bathroom first, the survey quick. He inched toward the bedroom, and Lincoln did his best to retreat farther into the darkness. If the light switched on it would be the end. There was no hiding, no true cover in the room. Clammy hands gripped tighter to his gun, his eyes blinking hard to clear the sweat dripping from his brow.

Just as the man entered the room, finger reaching for the light, his phone rang. He cursed quietly and removed the cell from his breast pocket. Slow steps slipped back into the living space. The line clicked over, though the voice on the other end went unheard from the shadows of the bedroom.

"He's here," the voice said. "Alone. Yes." Silence filled the room, the second man waiting patiently. Then the first nodded at the voice on the other end of the line. "Yes. Understood."

Dammit.

He had received confirmation of his orders. That might have meant any number of things, but they boiled to one thing: they were taking the Witness, either in cuffs or in a body bag. Lincoln could not allow that to happen—not before he had some answers.

Lincoln lifted his pistols, the first positioned for the man near the entrance. He stepped without a sound out of the bedroom and fired. The pistol boomed, the bullet piercing the man's forehead. He was dead before he hit the carpet.

The second pistol fired blind, Lincoln's focus still on the man closest to him. The bullet missed, a pinhole shot through the glass. Whistling wind wheezed into the room.

"What the hell?" the second shooter exclaimed. His gun was in his hand, but was too low to make a shot.

Lincoln was positioned, ready to end the conflict, which left the man only one play. He charged at Lincoln, screaming for his very life with each step. The shot slammed into his target's shoulder, to no avail. His momentum plunged him forward, barreling through his attacker like a tackling dummy at training camp.

Twin pistols scattered across the room, both lost in the struggle. Lincoln collided with the nearby wall, plasterboard caving from the pressure. The man continued to shout, using the adrenaline to ignore the bullet wound. Lincoln fought for leverage.

Since he was weaponless, his focus turned to keeping the man's pistol pinned to minimize the damage.

Hands cradling the man's wrist, Lincoln jerked it back hard. Bone snapped, and the gun fell to the carpet. Crying out in pain, the man staggered away from Lincoln. The agent took his advantage, leaping at the wounded figure. An arm reached around the man's throat, and the air was cut off from his lungs. He gasped, slamming his heel upon Lincoln's left foot.

Lincoln reeled back from the blow. The man turned to press the attack, but it was too late. Lincoln reached down, and one of the lost weapons slipped into his grasp. The bullet found its target and caught the man in his chest. He fell in agony, his eyes screaming then silencing to a vacancy never again to be filled.

Lincoln caught his breath. His sidearm hovered over both bodies as he searched for signs of life. He knew there were none. He was nothing if not efficient in his calling. It disgusted him to think in that regard; however, the truth lay at his feet for the world to see.

"Feel any better?" the Witness said with a wide grin. He clapped his approval of Lincoln's final decision.

Lincoln leveled his pistol on the man. "What did I say before?"

"I'm not sure, honestly," the Witness replied. "There was lots of heavy grunting involved, I'm sure. You did, however, save my life. Thanks to you, the future might have a chance."

"We'll see about that." Lincoln tucked away his pistol, then retrieved its twin as he wound his way back to the dead men cluttering the carpet. Crouching over the first, Lincoln patted the man's jacket.

"What are you doing?"

"Don't you already know? Isn't that your shtick?"

"Cute, Lincoln. Not an answer, but cute."

"I like to learn about the people I kill. At least their names, anyway."

"I wouldn't—"

"Wouldn't what?" Lincoln said, his hand inches from the man's breast pocket. The Witness remained motionless, the smirk gone from his lips. "What is it?"

The Witness pointed to Lincoln's chest, and the agent rose from the dead man. "Agent—"

A red dot danced along Lincoln's Kevlar vest. It shifted to his forehead. "What is—?" Before he finished his question, a phone rang. Not the hotel room or the burner at his side, but from the pocket of the dead man under his feet. Lincoln retrieved it. The sniper tracked his every movement.

The number was restricted on the screen, yet Lincoln answered the phone. A man's voice chimed through the speaker, though the winter wind caused static over the line.

"Stand. Slowly."

"Who is this?" Lincoln asked, following his instructions.

The voice chuckled. "It's funny how life turns out. This almost feels like old times."

Lincoln's eyes widened. The Witness caught his look. "I promised you answers, Lincoln. This is the first."

It was the man who had killed Morrison Engers—the man who had been at the other end of the sniper scope four years earlier. Recognition kicked in, disbelief swallowed for fact as the name tumbled from his lips.

"Marcus."

"I'd say it's good to see you, pal," Marcus Engers said. "But you never should have come back here."

CHAPTER EIGHTEEN

"It was during my second deployment."

She took a sip of coffee while she tried to figure out a path through the story. The beverage tasted sweet. The added flavor of the Styrofoam cup blended the drink to perfection.

Zac remained silent as she pondered the beginning of her story—one she had never shared previously. Not with Grissom, who had never pushed. Not with Riley, who asked much too often. Even Charlotte only knew pieces of the story, one that had ripped their family apart and continued to do so. Zac refrained from questions, merely a witness to her past.

"I was stationed at a medical compound in the middle of nowhere. Compound was a misnomer. It was just layers of tents along a cliff side close enough to a water supply to keep the staff from losing their minds, and far enough away from the front lines to keep the patients alive after surgery and hope they fully recovered. We were understaffed and overcrowded. Typical crap."

As a medical doctor, Morgan had had her pick of placements. Hard work throughout school had paid off, and she had jumped at the chance to implement the decade-long training. The field, however, was not as she'd hoped. Petty drama infected the medical profession. Petulant behavior from the staff on one end and money-grubbing administrators on the other had squeezed the life out of the job for her.

So she had enlisted—served a higher calling, hoping to make a difference to those truly in need.

"I was good at it," she said. "Great, in fact. I took the top spot within three months. Kept my patients alive with what I had, mostly my own sweat and whatever the convoys were able to drop off between patient transfers.

"Then, my brother showed up."

Morgan paused, waiting for a question. She hoped for a distraction, rather than continue down the path laid out by her past. Zac said nothing, waiting patiently through her hesitation.

The door down the hall remained closed. She wondered what was being said within—if Tyrese had opened his eyes yet and recognized the faces of his loved ones. Did he even consider them loved ones anymore or had he set about blaming them for his internal pain. Did he blame them for things they could never understand, never dreamt of knowing, because he never bothered to open up to them?

She should have been in the room, holding tight to Jamal and Charlotte. They were a family and should have been supporting each other. Instead, Morgan swallowed hard, pushing through her doubts, pushing through the pain of memory that swallowed up the joy.

"Ty joined the military for all the wrong reasons. He focused on the money and the benefits—on the education and job training available afterward. Not to say those are poor incentives, but to use them as your only reasons meant the work didn't matter. It was a means to an end.

"He didn't need any of it. Ty could have gone back to school to get all that. Money was never an issue. Our father's life insurance policy had provided more than enough to do whatever we wanted. It covered medical school for me. For Ty? He could have bought plenty of happiness.

"He joined up anyway. The bonus objective of keeping an eye on his little sis made for an easier decision. He was thinking about me instead of his own life. He never even considered the wife and kid he was leaving behind."

She put the cup down, hands straining along the edge of the bench. They blanched from the tension, tight along the wood. Anger rose at her brother, at his inability to trust her enough to take care of herself. She had never asked for a protector, never insinuated a need for him to join her, yet he had come regardless.

He paid for the decision.

Zac, reading her anger, reached for her. His hand settled

along her knuckles. "What happened to him, Morgan?"

She let out a long breath. "Routine surveillance went sideways, and he got caught in the crossfire. Took three rounds before someone pulled him to cover. By the time he arrived he was in bad shape. He got worse."

The convoy had brought in more than a dozen injured from the botched surveillance operation. She had worked through each in turn, never realizing her brother lay mere meters away. Injuries ranged from the most serious to those easily stabilized. Her brother lay in the middle; the longest second of her life passed when she recognized him beneath the blood and grime of war.

"I took care of the bullets."

"You?" Zac asked in surprise. "But—"

"He was my brother," she replied. "I wasn't going to leave anything to chance. I couldn't let someone else try and save him. The surgery went well enough, and I closed him up without issue."

She fell silent, though Zac was unable to follow suit. He filled the gap of her memory with the only outcome available. "He got sick."

Morgan nodded. "He needed meds to bring down a rising fever and for pain. We were almost out. Our convoys were never reliable. How could they be with everything going on? Ours never made it. I don't... I'm not sure what the official story was this time. If it was shot down at a previous stop, or maybe it was taken by hostiles en route to us—liberated by those who *really* needed it."

That had been the public perception overseas. That Americans had interfered in matters that did not concern them. They were simply the aggressors, fighting a losing battle on every front.

"Morgan..." Zac pressed. His voice was soft and compassionate, not a demand.

"I couldn't even tell him," Morgan said. "My brother. He was hardly lucid when he came out of the surgery, but by the time the news of the convoy reached us he was already in a coma."

Zac pointed down the hall, confused. "But he pulled through."

"He did."

He held his tongue for a long breath. She stood, letting the truth come, unwilling to look the man in the eye when the question came. And it had to come. There was no avoiding the end of the story. Not now. Not after everything.

"What did you do, Morgan?"

"I did what I had to, Zac!" Concern formed in the looks of those in the hall. They came from staff members unsure of their presence as well as grieving visitors checking in on loved ones. All paused in the wide corridor of the ICU.

Morgan leaned on the wall next to the bench, hands running through her hair. She tied the long black locks into a single tail, her chest heaving. Eyes closed, her voice softened, she continued, "I did what a sister would do for her brother."

Life without Tyrese had never been an option. She had refused to be the reason he died, not if there had been a chance in hell at saving him. And there had been one chance — though it came with a heavy price.

"There were three other patients under my care. Three, of four dozen at the time. They were taking the meds Ty needed. Meds that would save his life. I tried..."

Morgan closed her eyes and shook her head. The memory plagued her; it ate at her every waking thought. Returning to Baltimore, seeing Tyrese suffer, had cemented the sensation. It was one she had fought to share with the young man who wanted nothing more than to ease her burden.

He never pressed, never begged for the answer. Zac listened for her benefit, never his own. He was there for her and she appreciated the effort. He earned an answer for his patience.

"It was small dosages at first. I split them between all four, but it wasn't enough. I was losing him. So I made a choice."

"You chose your brother." She bowed her head. "You took the meds from the other patients."

"Yes."

"You saved your brother's life, Morgan."

"I watched *three* men die because of it." Tears fell down her cheeks. She swiped at them, each quickly replaced. "Men with families of their own. I made that choice, and I would damn well do it again."

"He found out, didn't he? Your brother?"

"I told him," Morgan confirmed. "When he was better and

smiling and laughing with his little sis, I told him the cost of my actions. He's barely spoken to me since."

"That's why…" Zac paused, rubbing his eyes. "Your medical license. Your discharge."

"Tyrese had me brought up on charges. I lost my commission as well as my license. I fell hard, but I found my footing eventually. Ty? He's just been falling."

Zac stood, joining her. "This isn't the first time?"

She shook her head. "Pills again. It wasn't too long after he came home. I tried to help at first. Tried to support him, but it was too late. Too late for us both. He screamed at me, blamed me for what he did, what he would do again. Just the sight of me, of having me in his life, did that to him. So I left. I ran from my family."

"Morgan, I didn't mean for this to happen. For you to—"

"You sent the text, Zac. Didn't you?"

A slight nod escaped him. "I took a peek at your personnel file a while back. I saw the list of relatives and I thought… I thought you should be here. That you'd want to be here."

She did, more than she realized. She missed her brother, missed the way they had made each other laugh growing up. She missed everything about their time together. Those days, however, were long gone. Now all that remained was pain, a pain she could never reconcile.

Morgan stared at the closed door separating her from her family. "I think I've done enough helping, don't you?"

CHAPTER NINETEEN

It was about Metcalf—the entire false front of an assessment to debate Ben's performance as a member of the DSA. None of it mattered to Stallworth, Sullivan, or the others gathered in judgment.

The others, though, gave Ben pause. They read their gathered findings and provided background to the drama, but remained locked on the table. Ben followed their reactions, noting how they responded to each of his answers. In turn, they muttered to their neighbor, their lips moving with nothing truly being said.

It was a play, a sham, and Ben was not the only puppet jerked around by strings dangling from the two overseers.

Sullivan rounded the table once more. "Now if we could discuss—"

Ben stood, causing the others to jerk upright in surprise. "I'm going to stop you there, Greg."

"I'm sorry?"

"Apology accepted," Ben said. His back ached from the hours of questioning, and the small pitcher of water had finally caught up with him. He ignored the pain and his full bladder, thin glare locked on his interrogators. "And I believe you heard me clearly enough."

"Agent Riley," Stallworth called from his position at the head of the table. "We have a *number* of items to get through."

"I'm sure you do," Ben said. "You should save them for the person they're actually meant for. Or is Director Metcalf not taking your calls?"

A shared glance between Sullivan and Stallworth ended the farce. Sullivan nodded to his colleague, and the latter silenced the recorder. "Yes. Very well."

Ben sat. His fingers ran the length of his bloodstained tie. "I could have done without the song and dance."

"We weren't sure."

Sullivan joined him on his end, pulling out a chair. "There was only so much we could glean from reports. You understand, don't you?"

"Not at all. There's a reason I'm at this end of the table. Frankly, I prefer it. It's more cut and dry. It leaves ambiguity out of the mix."

"Are you sure?" Sullivan asked. "You've entered a very ambiguous profession, Agent Riley. Do you know what side you're on?"

What sides were there? What game was being played? Part of what had kept Ben away from law enforcement, pushed him from his father's wishes for so long, was the idea of agendas outside of serving and protecting. To Ben there was only darkness and death down that road, where he sought to shine a light for people. But the DSA's world appeared darker than most, and the light faded more with each passing day.

"I get the feeling you'll be telling me the answer to that one."

"You've clearly figured out why we called you here."

Ben nodded. "Tell me anyway."

"Greg," Stallworth interrupted. A finger beckoned the deputy director over. "A moment?"

Sullivan pushed away from his chair, straightening his attire as he attended the private conference. Whispers escaped the pair, the observers refusing to even glance in their direction. When it ended, Sullivan stepped back from the table and gave the floor to his compatriot.

"Agent Riley," Stallworth began, "We have growing concerns over the work being undertaken by your peers, especially at the command level."

"Again, you should speak to Director Metcalf about those concerns."

"So we can listen to her lie to this Council?"

"Greg," Stallworth said, hand raised. Sullivan sighed and pulled back in deference. "Apologies. The deputy director, while overzealous, is not wrong. Susan has been less than forthcoming in the past. She has even disregarded her post in these sessions, distancing herself from the effectiveness of our coordinated efforts."

"Replace her, then."

"She carries some pull with certain members of our Council."

"Politics."

"Necessary where we are," Sullivan said with a shrug. "There are certain rules we must follow for what we have to do."

"What does that mean?"

"You said it yourself," Stallworth responded. He reached for a report at his side and opened the text. "Or typed it, rather. *This Witness character has a larger scheme. A long game being played. We have yet to put it together.*"

"You think Metcalf knows what it is?" Ben asked incredulously. The question echoed in the room. Stark silence fell from the men across from Ben, the truth written on their faces. "No. You think she's in on it. Seriously?"

Metcalf had sent the team to Bellbrook. She had authorized the mission to find seven thousand people. Why would she have done that if she already knew the reason for their disappearance? Why would she have sacrificed her team, knowing the signal's effects on people in the area?

Yet the information had come from within the DSA. Zac mentioned that stubborn fact during the briefing. Who had the access to use a backchannel server to notify them about the Bellbrook situation? Who had the wherewithal to manipulate events in that manner?

Metcalf certainly fit the bill.

"The simple fact is we aren't sure *what* Susan knows about recent events. She's hiding information, taking unscheduled trips and burying the objectives in the hopes we won't find out." Sullivan paced slowly, hand scratching his beard. "Bellbrook was merely one example. A recent one, but a compelling one nonetheless."

Stallworth cleared his throat. "We need your help."

"No."

Sullivan chuckled in surprise. "So quick to it? You're that loyal to a woman you barely know?"

"Agent Riley," Stallworth said. He passed along a folder to one of the nameless players in their meeting, who carried it over to Ben. "The director has had you under surveillance."

The folder slid under his waiting hand and he opened it. No words slipped from his lips. Cold eyes glanced at the photographs inside. There were images of his daily trip to the mall and his morning jogs. There were even more of Ben in his apartment. When he peered up, Sullivan loomed overhead. He caught Ben's reaction and grinned.

"You knew."

Ben nodded, closing the folder.

"Have you thought to ask why?" Sullivan pressed.

He pushed the file away. "It hasn't come up in the daily briefing."

"I knew you were smarter than that."

"Than what?"

"The part you play," Sullivan continued. "The sarcasm. The jokes."

"They keep me young."

"Or," the deputy director said, "it sets a certain level of expectation from those around you when you play the fool."

"Take it however you like."

"I will, thank you," Sullivan replied. The deputy joined him at the end of the table and reopened the folder. "You might not have been surprised by the images on top—those recent to your arrival at the DSA. But would you be surprised to hear they didn't start there?"

"What are you talking about?"

"See for yourself."

Images spread before him on the table. Multiple snapshots captured Ben in uniform. Not his shirt and tie routine with the DSA but his Buffalo PD blues. There were pictures of Ben on patrol, at the stationhouse, and even more when he had been at home with friends.

Sullivan leaned close. "Some of these photos go back years. Agent Riley, why would Susan Metcalf be monitoring your life?"

"I don't know."

"What has she told you about the house on Wex?" Sullivan pressed. "Do you know *why* your life was taken from you? Has she helped you find out any of the answers you've been searching for since your recruitment?"

They weren't wrong. Little progress had been made on his end. No help had come from the director. Then there were the surveillance photos. The images disturbed Ben. They fed into his paranoia, his growing distrust of the world he had been swept up in. At the same time, it made him relive the words of a maniac in the clearing of the great forest on the edge of Bellbrook.

There is a reason you are here. A reason you have been chosen by them, your so-called DSA.

There had been a reason Metcalf recruited him. She had known about him, followed him, and had tracked his every achievement and failure. Why? How had she come to choose his name above all potential candidates for the role?

Ben shook his head, unwilling to let the evidence swallow him whole. Unwilling to bend to the pressure laid before him. "I believe I said no thank you, gentlemen."

The members of the table turned toward him for the first time, all of them appearing to be surprised at the admission. He offered them a sad smile.

"Yeah... sorry, everyone. I'd prefer to chat with actual players in the conversation."

Stallworth met their silent stare before nodding to the men and women at the table. "We'll be along shortly."

Slowly, the others stood and moved for the door. Light showered the conference room. Ben refused to look away from Sullivan and Stallworth.

"Good," Ben remarked. "I could use a bathroom break."

The door closed and Sullivan leaned close. "Something is coming, Agent Riley. Bellbrook was just the start. This is bigger than we understand. If there is a chance Susan is involved we need to be ahead of it."

Ben waited, settling against his chair. "Finish."

"Excuse me?"

"Make your offer, Greg."

Sullivan pushed from the table and began pacing the length of the room. "Like I said. Smarter than you come off."

"We can give you your life back," Stallworth said.

Ben's eyes widened. "What?"

"This, your current job with the DSA, isn't what you want," Sullivan said. "We've reviewed the evidence against you. That house on Wex? Susan knew about it. She was monitoring it just as closely as she was watching you. Did she do a single thing to prevent your conviction? No. You lost everything, and she did nothing. What we are offering for your assistance is your life back. Fully restored, at the exact same position as when you left."

Stallworth rounded the table, joining them. "You will have no fear of reprisal, Agent Riley. No worry to you or your loved ones. You'll get it all back as if it never happened. The conviction will be overturned and buried. No questions asked."

"If I say no?"

"You won't," the assistant director to the NSA answered. "Agent Riley, you're a convicted criminal. All it would take is one call and —"

"That's not what we want to do," Sullivan interrupted, quick to cut off his associate. "None of us here wants to pose undue threats. No, I believe you'll help us because it is the right choice to make."

Sullivan slid a new report before Ben, hand resting heavily on the cardstock cover.

"What's this?"

"You mentioned something earlier about replacing Susan at the DSA," Sullivan said.

"Would it surprise you to know we tried that?" Stallworth finished.

"Nothing about you two surprises me right now."

"Yes, well, this might. A candidate was selected, and hearings were planned. Then, he was killed in the line of duty."

Sullivan's hands left the file, the label clear across the front of the thick report.

THE GRISSOM FILE

"Tell me, Benjamin. Do you know what actually happened to Agent Jacob Grissom?"

CHAPTER TWENTY
Des Moines - 2015

Morrison was preparing for his speech when it happened. In typical fashion, he had opened with a joke. It was a way for the man to relax against the rushing tide of comments from his aides about what tie best represented the audience, or where his eyes should fall with his opening sentence and when the most effective pause would be for applause. They were decisions outside Lincoln's purview, the choices amusing while also overwhelming and disconcerting in how they impacted the voting public once put together.

During moments like these, Morrison would break away from his prepared speech for a joke. Morrison always told the same type of joke. It had been a tradition of sorts with Lincoln. His jokes had never been for the faint of heart. Morrison had always pushed the envelope of good taste just to get it out of his system. It had been a way to put the pressure off him for a second and just laugh for a moment.

He never finished the joke. The bullet saw to that.

It punctured the window in a perfect circle. All fell to the ground, shocked and startled. Screams broke out, and panic filled the air. Every voice was focused on their personal safety. None realized the true target had gone silent in mid-sentence. None, except Lincoln, saw Morrison Engers catch the sniper's bullet to the chest.

A blur of motion followed. Lincoln turned away from the window at the sight of the senator falling. That slight shift saved Lincoln's life as a second bullet cut a hole through the glass and slammed into the agent's right shoulder. He collapsed from the impact and greeted the carpet with his face.

Over the roar of the people in the room, over the cries of the agents rushing onto the scene, a third shot rang out. No one fell, no one met their end from the bullet, and silence quickly returned to the suite.

Lincoln fought for breath. His eyes struggled to lock on a single target in the room. He caught a glimpse of the fallen senator and crawled toward him. Lincoln's shoulder was in agony as he pulled his body toward the unmoving figure.

Tears streamed down his cheeks, anger pushing him forward. Desperate hands searched for signs of life, but it was an unnecessary act. Morrison's chest never rose, and his eyes never blinked.

Lincoln should have said no. His tears were a recrimination of his decision. He should have stood by his concerns and his wariness over the abrupt trip to Iowa. Political ambitions be damned. None of that mattered now, ambition lost to the whims of the threats Morrison had failed to take seriously and Lincoln had failed to solve in time.

"Senator is down!" a man bellowed. The rest of the team scattered around the room. They assisted the staffers locked in the corners of the suite, who were all lost to shock and fear. "I repeat, the senator is down!"

A hand fell on Lincoln's shoulder. "Lincoln?"

The sobbing agent cradled the body of his friend. The smile faded from Morrison's face—every ounce of confidence and joy disappeared. Everything slipped away, the world a blur of sadness and loss.

"Lincoln?"

"Where?" Lincoln muttered. "Where did it—?"

"Rooftop," someone replied from the window. "A block over."

"Orders?" the agent at his side asked. "Lincoln?"

Lincoln swiped at his eyes. "I'll call it in. Get the locals for support."

"Are you—?"

"Go!" Lincoln shouted. The team ran from the room to coordinate the search pattern for the shooter. There was nothing he could do, no words he could say to make up for his mistake. All that remained was silence.

When he turned back to his fallen friend, the final resting place of the third bullet caught his attention. Lincoln stepped over to the wall and the single photo that had been shattered. It was the image of the senator with his son holding the golf trophy earned years earlier. It was taken long before he had entered into politics, before the days of pomp and pageantry. They had been just a father and son sharing the joy of a perfect day. The bullet had pierced the frame down the middle of the image, separating the boy from his father just as easily as the first shot had.

The day went as expected; the shooter was gone before teams managed to lock down the perch. Cordons on major highways were put in place, lockdowns at the train station and the airport.

All to no avail. The shooter had slipped through their fingers, the mission had been completed and the threats to a man of peace had finally been made real. Senator Morrison Engers, likely the next President of the United States, was dead.

Lincoln felt his heart through his chest. His entire body shook in the aftermath. The feeling refused to subside, carrying him from the Savery to the review panel months later. The pounding of his heart kept him from hearing the arguments placed against him, the blame thrown at his feet for what had happened in Des Moines. Someone had to own up to the error, and he couldn't deny his part in how things had happened. If only he'd pushed for more upfront time, or worked harder to determine who was threatening the senator's life. But he'd played the friend more than the protector. It was difficult to be anything else for Morrison; his charisma instantly won over a room.

The Service Review Board had no choice in the matter. The senator should have been protected at all costs. The blame rested with Lincoln. He simply stood in the room, listening to the cacophony in his chest, while a panel of his peers stripped him of his life. They took away his job, and with it, his purpose.

He lost everything.

When he blinked, more time passed. Four months. Gone in an instant. He hardly recalled them, stuck in a downward spiral that left him without a home or a cause to carry on. His only refuge was the Mission for Veterans in Washington, D.C. He had nowhere else to go and nowhere to belong.

Sitting on the stoop of the mission, Lincoln clung tight to his Medal of Distinguished Service from his time in Afghanistan, trying to remember a better time despite the pain it brought him. Lost in the past, he failed to detect a visitor approaching until his shadow blotted out the sun above.

"I heard about what happened." Marcus looked down at the broken man. Lincoln, through the haze of memory, was surprised at the strength and confidence displayed by the man wearing a pale suit. "I'm sorry, Lincoln."

"Marcus?" Lincoln asked. He stared at the young man in confusion. "I should be the one saying that."

"You did your job. My father… Well, he loved you like a son." Marcus stared off across the open lanes of highway, sadness in his eyes. His smile returned with him to the present. "What are you doing now? Here of all—"

"Figuring it all out," Lincoln lied.

Marcus nodded slowly, pointing to the medal in Lincoln's hands. "Heading back?"

"It was a thought," Lincoln said distantly. It was all he knew anymore. Loss and death. He tucked the medal aside and turned to Marcus. "I didn't see you after the funeral. Another secret endeavor?"

"You know me, pal," Marcus answered. "The group is always looking for good soldiers, Lincoln."

"Marcus, I…" Lincoln stopped and shook his head.

"I get it. I do." Marcus stood, brushing the dirt from his pants. The moment was lost for them. "Not all of us are built for war."

"No. We're not."

Marcus patted his shoulder lightly. "It seems to find us anyway, doesn't it?"

Lincoln watched Marcus leave, wondering if he would ever see the man again. He wondered if he would ever be able to see himself again for that matter. Lincoln was lost with no purpose to guide him. There were no great designs that his mother once saw for him—just the loss of the past and a future pulling farther and farther away from him.

"It always does, Marcus. It always does."

CHAPTER TWENTY-ONE

"It was you."

Lincoln squeezed the phone, his jaw clenched. The sun poured over the horizon. It reflected off the barrel of the sniper rifle positioned on the adjacent rooftop. The man lying behind the weapon remained still. It was a man Lincoln hadn't seen in years—not since the aftermath of his mistake.

"Come on, Lincoln," Marcus Engers said. "This isn't some Sunday-night teleplay on a third-rate cable station. Say what you have to say."

"All these damn years, Marcus," Lincoln fumed. "You killed your own father."

"Guilty."

Lincoln shook his head. He tried to shift, the red light following him closely until he stopped. "You disappeared. After that day at the shelter. I tried to reach out, to see how you were doing, but you were gone. You knew that was the end, didn't you? You were telling me the whole time and I couldn't hear you. Dammit, Marcus, I thought you were—"

"What?" the sniper laughed through the line. "The grief-stricken son? That was *your* role, wasn't it? The one you took from me. I found a new one thanks to you and dear old Dad. A true strength. Just like the senator always wanted."

The man's voice was cold and lifeless. He was as broken from the years as Lincoln had become. They were both simply going through the motions instead of finding true purpose in the world. Marcus sounded like he had nothing to live for, and that made him all the more dangerous.

Lincoln, however, was too busy thinking to recognize the

true danger of engaging with his potential killer. He was stuck on the memory from four years earlier when he lost everything he cared for in his life. That was when his surrogate father, his employer, and a man who stood poised to change the country for the better, died.

Murdered at the hands of his own son.

"The fundraiser was a setup."

"How else could I get Dad here? No politician passes on a donor fest and free food. Especially one poised to hit the national scene by announcing his candidacy."

"Why?"

"Really?" Marcus scoffed. "You have to ask? I would have done it long before that day. To tell you the truth, I thought about it that day you visited, when he first hired you. The way he spoke to me? It was like I was nothing. But I couldn't. The time wasn't right."

"Why this? Why now?" The questions came, but they were not aimed at the man on the phone. Instead, the Witness took a sharp breath and bowed his head.

His planning had brought them to this place—somewhere specific to Lincoln's past. Somewhere the answer to Morrison's death could come to light, because the Witness somehow knew Marcus would be the one brought in to clean up the situation. The enigmatic man played both sides against the middle.

"That's the best part," Marcus said. "This right here? Pure and total coincidence. A bonus for the brass."

"The Witness." Orders. Like the two men at Lincoln's feet, Marcus simply followed the orders of others. He served someone or something else entirely, something that controlled his actions.

"Agent MacKenzie," the spectacled man whispered. "Hang up the phone."

"Shut up," Lincoln snapped.

"He's a real charmer, ain't he?"

"Marcus, it doesn't have to happen like this. I'm bringing him in. He has answers I need."

"He has nothing, Lincoln," the sniper replied, his words sharp like the wind through the receiver. "Bringing him in isn't the objective."

Lincoln tightened his grip on the pistol at his side. It was useless against the threat of the sniper rifle, and he knew it. After everything, after all the preparation in the world, he was powerless. All he had left was his knowledge of the man at the other end of the barrel.

"Walk away, Marcus. I'm warning you."

Marcus laughed. "You are in no position to warn me, pal. I'm the one holding the gun."

"Take the shot, Marcus!" Lincoln shouted into the phone. He puffed up his chest. "This shot. Right here. It's what you've wanted to do for years, isn't it? The one you failed to do that day."

His shoulder ached at the admission. The bullet had pierced his right shoulder, through and through. It could have been much worse. It would have been a fatal shot if Lincoln hadn't turned at the last possible second, instinct kicking in at the sight of his falling friend.

Two centimeters. Two measly centimeters and the bullet would have clipped his right subclavian artery, causing him to bleed out on the carpet next to the man who had taken him in and given him a life, a home, and a family he thought lost to him forever.

"Do it already," Lincoln repeated. "Take the shot. Show us what kind of killer you really are."

"Agent MacKenzie," the Witness said. He peered at the watch on his wrist. "You need to listen to me."

"What kind of killer I am?" Marcus said through the static on the line. "I'm not the villain in this. You just have to look at the two men on the floor to see that. Difference between us? I don't kill indiscriminately."

"Marcus—"

"Eleven seconds, Lincoln," the Witness persisted, his voice louder this time. "Do you hear me? Ten, nine..."

"A soldier follows orders, Lincoln," Marcus said. "You used to know that."

"Six, five..."

"You're no soldier, Marcus," Lincoln answered. "You're just a punk-ass kid with daddy issues."

"DROP!"

Lincoln did. The Witness tipped sideways along the chair before rolling to the carpet. Glass shattered overhead and whipped along the wind, crashing into the room with each shot fired. Marcus unloaded on the room, screaming as he unleashed hell on the hotel suite. There was no control in the act—only the tantrum of a child.

Scurrying to find cover, Lincoln used the dead men at his feet as a shield. He lost sight of the Witness in the chaos, his eyes closed to block the flying debris.

The back of the chairs disappeared under Marcus' barrage. The conversation was lost to violence, and the world turned into a blur of rage and memory. Half in the moment, half in the past, Lincoln's vision faded, unsure of reality anymore.

He had come to this moment hoping for closure, hoping to walk away from the violence infecting his every thought. Instead, he had opened the door to more—more death and more loss.

"Marcus..."

Other than the blistering wind raging through the suite, silence returned. Lincoln opened his eyes, pushing away the dead man. He struggled to his knees. His hands ran the length of his body for signs of injury. A sigh of relief escaped him.

"Damn you, Lincoln." Marcus' voice rang out from the phone. The line crackled with static, and then it went dead.

A single shot shattered the newfound peace. Hands and knees gave way, forcing Lincoln down to the carpet once again.

He waited, the seconds ticking by in his mind. This was his life, the same as it had been that day at the bridge when he lost his mother. His entire existence had been surrounded by violence and death. Nothing could ever change that, try as he might. Marcus had made that much clear.

Time passed, though Lincoln could no longer tell whether it was only a minute or an hour. He inched back to his knees. Each move was careful to stay out of view from the rooftop across the street.

No sniper scope tracked his movements as he reached for the cracked door frame to the bedroom. Lincoln edged to his feet, then stopped. The two dead men stared at him and he returned to their bodies, finishing the search begun before the hailstorm of bullets.

A badge slipped from the jacket pocket of the man with the gaping hole between his eyes. Lincoln bit his lip, hesitant to open the billfold for confirmation of his worst fears.

LT. SCOTT MARSHALL - ARMY INTELLIGENCE

"Did you know about this?" Lincoln said, eyes flailing about the room. "Cause for a damn witness you're—"

Gone. The Witness was gone. In the desperate scramble for cover, in his fear of facing Marcus' wrath, Lincoln had lost sight of the target. Not a shred of clothing from the man's pristine suit was present. There wasn't a footprint in the bloodstained carpet, not a trace to suggest he had even been in the room.

Only the note card tucked on his former chair remained: the one that had been present throughout their discussion. The one the man had refused to share until the time was right.

"How?"

Lincoln retrieved the card, reading through the casually scrawled missive.

I promised you answers and delivered, Lincoln. You need me. More than you know. Two friendly pieces of advice before you call the number at the bottom of this message:
    1. Don't tell Agent Dunleavy the truth.
    2. Don't forget to turn around.

The beaten and battered agent read through the card twice more before he jammed it into his pocket. After everything, Lincoln lost the man—he lost the link to the answers he needed and now had nothing to show for his efforts.

No. Not nothing.

Don't forget to turn around.

Bullets riddled the far wall of the suite. It had been an exercise in rage, not the way of a soldier on a mission. It wasn't the work of a highly trained soldier as much as it was an angry kid throwing a tantrum.

Only it wasn't.

The plaster had taken the hits. Only the wallpaper lay in tatters, not the photos decorating the surface. Except for one image. If Lincoln was a betting man he would have wagered his entire life the final bullet, that final statement on the mess of this mission, had landed in the shattered photo.

The Red Bridge in downtown Des Moines.

Marcus had left a calling card, telling Lincoln where they would meet again.

For the last time.

CHAPTER TWENTY-TWO

Hours passed. Time better spent in a dozen different areas was relegated to the confines of the break room. Stir crazy was not a concept known to Metcalf, a woman at ease working twenty-hour days without suffering from exhaustion. The confinement at Fort Meade, however, tested her both mentally and physically.

Diversions assisted in passing the time. Hourly updates from department heads allowed her to keep a hand on the daily operations of her department. There was nothing from Zac, a definite concern after witnessing his conversation with Sullivan earlier, but Adler—a wise addition to her team—stepped up to the plate to deliver all relevant data.

Stephanie joined her at times, providing moral support as well as company for an impromptu meal from the vending machines. Little was said about the meeting unfolding across the hall. There were a few complaints over Martin eyeballing the woman's every move along the corridor. Beyond that, though, little could be said.

They didn't know anything.

That was what it boiled down to: the unease of the unknown, which brought down the ever-prepared director. Out of her element, Metcalf let the time pass without a fight.

With the fading of the sun came the scrambling of steps in the hall. Metcalf peered outside the small window beside the break room door. Men and women vacated the conference room, shuffling in silence down the wide corridor for the inner workings of the NSA.

She recognized some of them, analysts on par with the dozens working in her hub thirty miles away. Low-level employees, none considered high profile enough to be included in a meeting with the members of the Inter-Agency Council.

"What the hell?" Metcalf opened the door, shifting between the departing members of the NSA while the question raged on her lips.

Kanigher cut her off, blocking the way to the doors and the three shadows remaining within.

"Let me through, Bobby."

"They will be out momentarily, Susan," Kanigher replied. "Let's not make a bigger issue out of this. Please."

Metcalf bit her lip, then settled along the far side. Her eyes locked on the door. She refused to even blink for fear of missing something more than she already had, which turned out to be considerable. Seconds slipped to minutes, and then the shadows of the conference room returned. Stallworth exited for the hall, tall and proud.

"Donald," Metcalf called. "What the hell have you done?"

Stallworth said nothing, his loathsome smirk enough of a response for the frantic director. He joined the others of his organization, Kanigher and Martin providing a buffer from the questioning bystander left behind.

"Now, Susan..." Sullivan said, with his hands extended in front of his chest. His words were calm and soft, a tone that did nothing to appease Metcalf's anger. She rushed the deputy director, snatching his collar with both hands. She slammed him back against the wall.

"What the hell is going on here?"

Sullivan waited until she released her grip. He straightened the shirt beneath his signature sweater vest and smiled. "An assessment of Agent Riley. As I said."

"Bullshit," she snapped. "An assessment for you and Stallworth, yet no one else? Since when are meetings held without all members present?"

"Since Agent Grissom was lost to us."

Metcalf reeled back a step from the name. It always came back to Jacob Grissom. It was her decision that had led to his death. No matter the justification, no matter the conversations held between them in secret over their search for the truth behind the work of the DSA, there was no coming back from that decision.

It was the right call, and she was forced to live with the fall-out. Grissom needed her to continue, to make sure his sacrifice hadn't been in vain, for the sake of the DSA and for the country. Metcalf had to carry the torch in more ways than one, and now it unraveled before her.

Thanks to Greg Sullivan.

"You have a problem with my ability to head my department, you tell me," Metcalf said. "You don't bring Stallworth into it. Or my subordinates."

"You have to admit things have not been right since the loss of my predecessor."

"No. I don't." Metcalf turned away. The very sight of the man irritated her to no end. "Damn you for bringing this here. You should have brought your concerns to me and only me."

"I did," Sullivan admitted easily. "You chose to ignore them."

Metcalf's eyes burned. "What is this about, Greg? Feeling your age? Are you just looking for a raise, or is my chair really so much more comfortable?"

Sullivan scoffed. "As if that has any appeal to me."

"No," Metcalf continued, tracking his gaze, trying to get a read on the man who pretended to be one with her cause. "It's about the show of it, isn't it? You hate the DSA. The secrets, the half-truths, the hiding in the shadows. Not for Greg Sullivan, former congressman from nowhere. I'll tell you once and only once, Greg. Find your spotlight elsewhere."

Sullivan nodded, then leaned close. "This, Susan. *This* is why they cut you out."

"You mean Stallworth."

"For now. But how long until he brings them up to speed?"

"On what?" she yelled. "For what?"

"Bellbrook was a mistake," Sullivan said. "Chicago was another. Don't pretend we don't know where you've sent Lincoln MacKenzie. I know what you're really looking for at the DSA. Those answers hidden in the dark should stay there, Susan. For your sake and for the sake of your beloved department."

He had played her, used her, for this moment. Every report, every error, had been catalogued and turned against her no matter the context.

"You son of a bitch."

"Me?" Sullivan said. "No, Susan. I'm the best friend you have right now. They want your head. One more screw up, one more secret and—"

"Enough."

Sullivan smiled, hands outstretched. "I am trying to help."

"Yourself," Metcalf said.

The sound of footsteps silenced them. Ben stood in the open doorway of the conference room. *How long had he been there?* Metcalf nearly cried out. He appeared exhausted, dark circles under his usually joyful brown eyes. He hesitated for a moment after being discovered, then moved toward the exit.

"Agent Riley."

Ben failed to glance back, to offer any form of reply. He simply clutched tight to a thick file trapped against his side.

"I suggest giving the young man some time," Sullivan said.

"What was it, Greg?" she asked, tracking her wayward agent. "What did you give him? What line?"

"Only the truth."

"And the file?"

"He deserves to know what happened. The cost of your leadership."

The Grissom File. It was her greatest failure as director. "How could you? I—"

"Let him go, Susan." Sullivan backed away from her, a satisfied smirk across his face. "Frankly, you have larger concerns at the moment."

He turned to follow the other members of the covert meeting, no doubt to update Stallworth over their latest conversation. The game that was being played astounded her and confused her at the same time. If it wasn't about her position then what was it? If the DSA wasn't the endgame, what was? How did it relate to turning Ben against her?

Stephanie rushed to her side. "What happened? I passed Agent Riley, but he wouldn't even look at me."

"They told him about Grissom."

The assistant's eyes widened. "Want me to talk to him?"

"No." It needed to come from her. She had put it off for too long, put too much distance between everyone. "Thank you though."

Stephanie nodded. "I'll bring the car around."

Alone in the corridor, Metcalf cursed quietly under her breath. Sullivan had used the members of the Council against her. He'd made unilateral decisions, prodding her in a specific direction, forcing her into this position.

Through her ignorance, she had allowed it.

CHAPTER TWENTY-THREE

Despite everything—the pain of dredging up her past and the guilt over the deaths of three innocent men to save one—Morgan stayed. Zac supported whatever decision she made, leaving her to return to the office and the pile of work waiting for him.

She sat in silence in the aftermath, questioning everything. Part of her wondered how long it would take to reach her car, to slam the Impala into drive and blast onto the highway. She could put Baltimore, Tyrese, their shared childhood, and every other bad memory in the rearview, just as she had since her recruitment to the DSA. It was a happy dream, one lost to the silence surrounding her.

Visitors left in waves, the hours dwindling for their presence. Morgan tried to keep her eyes away from their worried gaze and their concern for loved ones. They clearly wondered if they would be here tomorrow—knowing some would not.

She huffed, leaving the discomfort of the bench for the water fountain around the corner. A small sip soothed the burning in her throat. When she returned to the hall and the closed door of Tyrese Dunleavy, the room was empty. Charlotte and Jamal were hurrying down the corridor, hand in hand.

It was time for her to make a decision. She had come all this way at the drop of a text, subconsciously knowing what she would find waiting for her. To leave without a word, to run away from the life she missed to her core, was a disservice.

A nearby nurse nodded at her questioning glare, thanks passing from Morgan's lips before she approached the waiting door. The handle was a boulder in her path she fought to move, before it finally allowed her entrance to the darkened space.

The quiet faded to the sound of beeping and pulsing monitors. She scanned them quickly, ignoring the body in the middle of the room. The heart rate was strong, especially considering the effects of the overdose. Blood pressure was well within range. EKG offered another glimpse of hope at the outcome once the drugs were filtered from his system.

Tyrese. His cheeks were gaunt, withered from age. His once muscular frame had dwindled since her departure, the need for strength no longer an imperative. He appeared ill — sick and lost in the world — and it was her fault. Instead of pushing through the guilt, Morgan turned for the door, her visit nothing more than her own reminder.

"You *are* here."

She stopped, head low. Tyrese's deep eyes fluttered open. He struggled to sit up. A grateful smile grew along her lips.

"I… I'm glad to see you're awake, Ty."

He said nothing, and she offered the same in return. They settled into each other's company, struggling for a way into the other's life though unsure of how to proceed. His discomfort was prominent, and she moved to help, only to be rebuffed by his rising hand. Morgan paused, realizing the act answered her question about whether or not he wanted her to stay in the room. She backed away for the waiting corridor and the long trek home. The handle twisted under her pressure and the door eased from the frame.

"Is that it?" Tyrese called, locking her in place once more. "That's all you came to say? No speeches from the high and mighty Morgan Dunleavy?"

"I didn't think that would be necessary this time."

"They were never necessary. Didn't stop you before though."

Morgan's fists clenched at her sides. Her teeth dug deep into her lower lip. She inched the door to the frame, the solid pine never latching. "I didn't come for a fight."

"Then why did you?" he asked in anger — the same anger she heard in every discussion after the war. "To show me how much stronger you are than me? To tell me how much better your life is? That there are no nightmares dogging your every step? That you have no regrets over what happened?"

"What happened? You mean what I did, don't you? What *I* did, Ty."

Tyrese shook his head. "You still feel nothing."

Her hand slammed against the end of the bed. "That is crap and you know it. They were my patients. They put their lives in my hands and I…" Morgan closed her eyes and held her breath. A second passed, then three, before her heart started to slow. Her saddened gaze fell on her brother. "No. I won't do this with you. Not here."

"All this time and you still won't face it."

"At least I live with it!" she snapped. "What is running away going to prove?"

His arms struggled to cross his chest. "You know nothing about me."

"I don't have to," Morgan said. "I see that young man out there, the boy that lives and breathes for his dad, and I don't need to know anything else. You should feel the same."

Tyrese turned for the window. "I'll get better. I'll be better. I can get help."

He refused to look at her to say it directly. Morgan shook her head in disbelief. "I'm not your wife, Ty. I'm the only one who can see through your crap. You've been that way ever since grade school when you told Mrs. Henderson your sob story about your missing homework. I know how convincing you are. But you need help. Charlotte and Jamal need you to get help. I need you to—"

"You done?" Tyrese spat. "I said I would."

Pain rested in his eyes, any light from outside swallowed up by his wide pupils. Morgan stepped in front of him, demanding his full attention. "Damn you, Ty. What is it going to be next time? More pills? You damn coward. They came in here with hugs and kisses like you were the victim. Like *you* were the one with bruises hidden on your skin."

"Get the hell out."

"No," Morgan answered without hesitation. She was unwilling to let it go any longer. Unwilling to leave anything unsaid this time. "You don't need coddling. You need a damn beating. You think I'm afraid to face what I've done? I live with it every day. I suffer for it. You saw to that."

"You were wrong to make that choice."

"I saved your life. And you'd just throw it all away."

"Three people died!" Tyrese yelled. A nurse started for the

door, though she was held back by Morgan's insistent glare. Tyrese calmed, his head deep in the pillows. "I can't—"

"What happened back then is on me. Those lives are on me, not you."

"I know," he said, the anger welling up. "You betrayed everything and you don't even see it! We may not have been the most spiritual people on the block, Morgan, and church was never one of our hot spots, but we sure as hell believed in the Lord enough to understand right from wrong. You forgot that."

Morgan took the punches from every condemnation, letting them sink through her hardened shell. No tears flowed down her cheeks. She refused to let them, not in front of her brother.

"No," she replied. "I made a choice. There was no right answer, and I paid for it. I lost everything. Including you."

"You should have let me decide, Morgan. Those men had families of their own. Death follows us everywhere we go because of what you did. I can't live like that."

"Ty…" She reached for him and he pulled away.

"Now kindly get the hell out."

The beeping of the monitors filled the room. Morgan circled the bed for the door. The handle was cold to the touch. She paused, tear-filled eyes turned toward the huddled mass of a man she had done everything she could to save. He was her greatest sacrifice and failure wrapped in one.

"Find a way, Ty," she said into the darkness, unsure if her words penetrated his anger. "Not for me, but for your family. Always for them."

CHAPTER TWENTY-FOUR

She struggled to breathe after the door closed. Keeping her back to the glass, unwilling to appear weak in front of her brother, Morgan stood tall even as the tears slipped from her eyes. Every burden threatened to crash down upon her aching shoulders, and every muscle was exhausted from the exchange. She fought through them, shuffling away from the darkness of Tyrese's room.

No words remained. They fell on deaf ears. He heard none of it: none of her guilt, none of the nightmares that plagued her or the pain at the lives taken by her choice.

He placed the entire situation at her feet, including the aftermath. Everything was her fault, from the bruises on his wife's body to Tyrese's suicide attempts. Would his next attempt finally end his pain? Was it even about his pain anymore? Or was it just about forcing Morgan to face the error of her decision?

Three lives for one. Who knew what great feats those men could have achieved had they survived? What children were denied the world thanks to her selfishness? What voices were silenced by her inability to say goodbye to her brother?

Morgan closed her eyes, wondering if the pain would ever abate, if there was a way to silence the past for a breath—a single second to gain some peace in the world.

"Morgan."

Charlotte approached slowly, hands fumbling nervously before her. Jamal rested uncomfortably on a nearby bench, the day clearly having taken its toll. Morgan's eyes flitted away from the pair. Her fingers quickly swiped at her cheeks.

"I'm leaving, Charlotte," she replied. "Just like you asked."

Charlotte's hand fell on Morgan's, clutching tight. "Wait. Please?"

"Why? You want to curse me out again? Maybe show me how much I've hurt your family with my actions?" The beeping of the monitors filled her ears. The sight of the huddled form of her defeated brother struggling to find his way back into the world was locked in her memory. Morgan shook her head. "No need."

"That's not—" Charlotte stopped, pulling her aside. "Please, Morgan. I didn't know you were in there, and I was heading back in to see him again. I never meant to overhear but... I heard what Ty said."

"Feel like adding to it?"

"Dammit, Morgan," spat her sister-in-law. "Just shut your mouth for a second."

Morgan fell silent and leaned against the wall. Charlotte struggled for the words, arms crossing her chest. Her back straightened, the weariness fading and the confidence of Morgan's long-time friend returning.

"I love him," she started. "I loved him the second I saw him in that stupid cheerleader costume he wore that one Halloween."

"Not the best story to share with Jamal," Morgan muttered. A glare shot her way and she accepted it with a wave. "Sorry. My new partner must be rubbing off on me." Another glare, and Morgan sighed. "Never mind."

"I just meant that Ty makes me whole," Charlotte continued. "His eyes. His hands. His smile. To imagine a world without him is my personal hell."

"Mine too."

"I know. I know that now more than ever." Charlotte reached for her, fingers grazing along her arm. "You saved him. He can't see that. Not with everything that happened. But I see it. No matter the pain, and no matter what we suffer as a family. We do it because of the opportunity you gave us. And I never thanked you for that."

Morgan took her friend's hand in her own. It had been years since they confided in each other—years shattered by heartache and pain. Morgan had tried to make things right, tried to support her family, but only served as a painful reminder of their inherent weakness.

Charlotte had lashed out at who she believed to be the cause of the conflict and the source of her marital struggles. Neither had actually spoken to each other about what happened, allowing Tyrese to narrate their dissolution without a chance to make things right.

Morgan was thankful for the chance, grateful to hear her friend's words at last. Then her gaze fell on the bruises dotting the young mother's skin, wounds that reminded them both of the cost of their silence. They were the cost of Morgan's decision, despite her intentions.

"You never have to thank me," she whispered. Charlotte extended her sleeve. "Char, I don't deserve your thanks."

"Yes you do," she answered. "I can see that now. What happened overseas? What you both went through and the choice you had to make? You can pretend to be strong through it all but I see it in your eyes. They are the same as his."

"Charlotte—"

"We can help him. We *will* help him. But only because you gave us the time. Don't forget that."

Time was all they held now. It was a chance at better days ahead, a hope for light to re-enter the man's life and take residence in his heart. It was a chance to watch his son grow to adulthood, for Tyrese to age next to his beautiful bride, and for them all to share incredible adventures or simply enjoy each other's company in the comfort of their home.

She gave them that opportunity. It had been at a cost, to be sure, but the choice was made and she would live with it—swallow up the nightmares and continue as she had for so long already.

"I won't," Morgan said, wiping her tears.

Charlotte pulled her close in a hug, the first they had shared in years. Both laughed to force the pain away for a time, knowing it would return eventually. They knew they would be there for each other to fight it back again.

When they parted from the hug, Morgan started to leave—the late hour more than a sufficient excuse for her departure. Instead, Charlotte took her hand and escorted her to the waiting bench and the tired form of Jamal, who struggled to keep his eyes open.

Morgan held him close, the youth excited for the chance to be with his aunt. She listened to every change in his life: school, girls, sports, and comic books. He spoke of everything from the mundane to the extraordinary, though little sparked Jamal as the former. To him, all stood as exceptional, and for a time under the humming lights of the ICU at Mt. Sinai, Morgan Dunleavy believed him to be correct.

They spoke for hours, joking and laughing. Eventually, time slipped away from them as it always managed to do. Charlotte and Jamal returned to the darkened room and their patient. They entered stronger than they had been earlier. Morgan carried that same hope with her as she exited the hospital.

It was a hope for her brother's recovery and a confidence in making it work this time. There would be no more running away, no more self-exile from those she cared about. No more distance.

As the hospital faded behind her, whispered a prayer for Tyrese to survive. That was all they had ever done in life, ever since the loss of their parents. They were Dunleavys. No matter the heartache, no matter the obstacle in their way or the night-mares at their back.

They survived.

CHAPTER TWENTY-FIVE

The Red Bridge stood only fifteen feet above the water of the Des Moines River. Lincoln paused at the west-side approach of the once proud train route of the nineteenth and twentieth centuries. Since being shuttered in its original intent, the bridge now served as a simple trail for pedestrians, though the opening of Principal Riverwalk to the north had cut the trail's foot traffic down substantially.

It was a plus for Lincoln, who continued to search the area for surprises. Marcus had come to Des Moines with two other individuals holding government IDs. Lincoln had no way of knowing whether or not Marcus was now alone or if more back-up waited in the wings.

Every instinct, however, screamed otherwise. Marcus was not prone to think through situations. He wasn't able to prepare to the extent Lincoln had through his multiple tours overseas.

The wary agent used his scanning as an excuse. The bridge itself loomed in front of him, and the sound of choppy water dotted by sheets of ice kept his feet locked in position and his old fear in full control.

You are strong enough, even now. You let fear take over, and it ain't never giving up its grip. You understand?

His mother's words pushed him ahead—driving him to the unknown on the bridge. There was no other way to learn the truth. He had to see it in Marcus' eyes. He needed to understand where everything went wrong and how to fix it—to find a way to put it all behind him and move on.

His foot fell on the walkway, followed by another step along the bridge. Each was hesitant. Lincoln closed his eyes, his mother at one side, Captain Thomas at the other. They forced him to stand, to step deeper into the shadows over the Des Moines River. Morrison and Ruth joined them from behind, their combined strength pouring through him.

He couldn't let them down. He couldn't let a simple fear win out over his need — and his need was great. The truth was finally in reach. Closure had been the main objective of his travel to Iowa. He had found it in the most curious of ways thanks to the man he was sent to kill.

Lincoln held tight to his pistol. Thin streams of moonlight broke through the dark, swirling clouds overhead and glinted off the barrel. It lit his way, guided him along the bridge and over the flowing ice, the cold death of the water waiting underneath.

The winter pressed into him. The wind blasted from the far side of the bridge, and drove him back. Lincoln squinted against the elements as he continued farther into the center of his fear. He had a job to do and nothing would stand in his way.

Marcus stood in the shadows near the railing. He stared out over the water, obviously unafraid of Lincoln's approach.

"I didn't think you would come," Marcus said.

"Here I am."

"Good," he replied. "I've wanted to end this for a long time, pal."

Marcus turned to greet his former superior. He was no longer the skinny son of a prominent senator, no longer the ambitious dreamer looking to make a headline instead of fighting for a cause — the figure before Lincoln had been transformed.

Gone were Marcus' flawless features, the poster boy bent on political aspirations like his father before him. The right side of his face rippled like burnt skin from his cheek all the way down his neck. His arms were built, the veins underneath threatening to burst. His muscular legs stretched his camouflaged pants. A green light beamed from beneath the man's tight shirt, center to his chest. Wires snaked out along his skin. The ticking of circuits echoed in the silence of their greeting.

Lincoln barely felt his fingers in the cold. The freezing wind cut through him, though he wore gloves and three layers of clothing. Marcus, however, approached with little more than a workout outfit. No breath fogged before him, and no goosebumps ran along his flesh. He stood as if more machine than man, causing Lincoln to fall back a step, afraid for the stranger standing before him.

"Marcus?" he asked, suddenly seeking confirmation, unsure of the figure looming on the bridge. "What have you done?"

"I built myself for war, Lincoln." It was in his sneer, despite the deformed portion of his once pristine face and the deeper voice rising from his throat, which sold his identity to Lincoln. Marcus carried a wide, knowing grin, like he owned the board and everyone else played a game of his design. "I gave myself the strength you always demanded. Aren't you proud of me?"

CHAPTER TWENTY-SIX

"Don't you like my new look?"

Marcus' glib tongue amid the horror marking his face continued to shock Lincoln to silence. For all the violence he had seen over the course of his life, for all the death, destruction, and pure contempt for humanity shown during his time in the military and beyond, Lincoln had never witnessed such self-infliction of pain.

Marcus had held the world in his hand, wealth and power thanks to his father's position. Everything had fallen in line for him, including a bright future. Now, it had been thrown away.

"Marcus..."

"Do you know what they tell you?" Marcus read the concern and smiled, though the action was misshapen from the bubbling skin along his right cheek. "They tell you it's a small adjustment at first. A clarity of vision. Muscle-enhancing drugs to strengthen the core, arms, and legs. They give you injections to increase blood flow and cognitive function, allowing more fluidity for the synapses. All to make you the perfect soldier."

An abomination, Lincoln thought. That was all he saw in Marcus. "What the hell are you talking about?"

"What am I talking about?" Marcus huffed. He pointed to his right eye, bloodshot and intense. The lids appeared to have been surgically removed. "This! All this! It was meant for you."

That was the great opportunity Marcus had tried to offer him years ago. He phrased it as a potential career—a new and more purposeful mission in life. All of it had been a lie.

"My old man stepped in and pulled you away before I finished," Marcus continued. "I thought I could win you over, make you understand the importance of the work the group was doing. But you rejected me. When my father shunned me, traded up for a better son? I volunteered."

"Your secret endeavor."

"The very same," Marcus confirmed. "It wasn't nearly ready when I first mentioned it. There were kinks to work out and research to finalize. They never wanted me though. Can you believe it? All that, building up this decision, placing myself in their hands, yet they didn't even want me for the job. I was a means to an end. I was money for their coffers—they could use the Engers name to sell the project to potential customers. Everything I had, and I wasn't good enough. Just like with the old man, they wanted you."

"I never would have joined."

"I knew that," Marcus said. He snapped his fingers, hand swirling in a broad arc, always grazing the pistol at his side, but never pulling it free from the holster. "Deep down I always knew that. Even at the shelter, when you had nothing left, I saw the arrogance in your eyes. You call it strength, but it wasn't. You always thought your way was so damn righteous compared to mine. I wanted to change the world. But it turned out all they wanted was a gun to control."

"Who?" Lincoln pressed. He reached for Marcus, who retreated farther into the shadows. "Dammit, Marcus, who did this to you?"

"I did this to myself!" the enhanced soldier screamed. "When they rejected me I took their drugs. I followed the regimen, building up my body to show you, to show dear old Dad I could stand on my own. I would be stronger, faster, smarter than his chosen son."

That day at the airport. Marcus had appeared different—larger, more confident than Lincoln had ever known him to be. Words hadn't been said, and none had been necessary after Marcus' handshake threatened to break Lincoln's hand. If only Lincoln had asked, if only either of them realized the strength their words carried, none of this would have been necessary.

"It didn't matter," Marcus said. "I wasn't sure how to act when you showed up in Des Moines. I wasn't ready to take the shot, but when I saw you two approach, his hand on your shoulder like family? You may as well have called it then. You killed him just as much as I did, Lincoln."

"Don't you dare try to pin that on me," Lincoln snapped. "You made a choice."

"So did you."

"Who did this? Who made this possible?"

"Unreal," Marcus scoffed. "The level of stupidity you display. You're DSA. You know all about Asset Control."

Lincoln's brow creased. His head shook at the accusation laid at his feet. *Asset Control?* "I don't. I don't know any of it, Marcus. That's not what the DSA is about."

Marcus laughed, booming and hollow at the core. "Is that what they told you? What he told you too? The Witness?" Marcus pointed at the Savery in the distance, less than a mile over yet hidden by the Des Moines skyline. "Nothing about losing time or the damn cryo ward? About sacrificing my life for the program because of what I did?"

"No. None of it, Marcus," Lincoln said. He held his breath, and tried to calm his nerves. Each exhale slowed his pulse, and he lowered the volume of his voice in an effort to contain the situation. "Talk to me. Tell me why you're after the Witness."

"Weren't you listening?" Marcus' eyes flared in anger, his pupils sucking in what little light resided along the bridge. "He knows what's coming! He pushed the timetable, started events none of us can control. That scares the crap out of them."

"Why?"

"He wants to stop it, but he can't. No one can. And freelancers aren't appreciated by the US government." Marcus' fist clenched, slamming against his side. "I had him, Lincoln. I finally had my chance to be rid of this burden, to be free of them. It was penance for my mistakes, for killing my old man too soon. They wanted him to announce his candidacy that day. They wanted a man in the Oval Office. Kane and the others had planned it for decades and I messed it up for them. I didn't know. I was so damn angry. Because of you, Lincoln. What you took from me. What you keep taking from me!"

"Me?" Lincoln asked in shock. Plans for Morrison? Marcus' group had been manipulating Morrison to gain access to the White House? Who were these people and why would Marcus get in bed with them? Unfortunately, none of his questions cut to the true heart of the matter. Through it all, through the murder of his own father at his hands to the destruction of his own body, the blame had never fallen to Marcus. It always came back to Lincoln. "Dammit, Marcus, I saved your life! I've never done anything except try to keep you and your family safe. I had nothing to do with what happened to you."

"You had *everything* to do with it!"

"Talk to me, Marcus. This isn't you. It couldn't be you. Tell me how to fix this. We can put a stop to this. Together."

"You're a damn fool, Lincoln. There is no stopping what's coming. It's about leveraging what we control before we lose everything. Trust me on that, pal."

"I can't," Lincoln replied, his words lost in the wind. "I wish I could Marcus, but I can't."

"I know," Marcus said. His pistol was immediately in his hand, the movement a blur. Marcus leveled the weapon on his target, a sad smile on his face. "That's why it ends like this."

CHAPTER TWENTY-SEVEN

Lincoln hated being right. When he had arrived in Des Moines thirty-six hours earlier there had been only one path to take, one road into the future. Kill the Witness, find closure for Ruth, and bring peace to the thousands dead in Bellbrook. The end of the story.

Violence for violence's sake. The only thing Lincoln ever truly excelled at in life. Death and loss. When the Witness had offered him a choice, a way out of the vicious cycle that infected him to the core, Lincoln balked. He had kicked and screamed, fighting to maintain his natural tendency, to stay on the path laid out since that fateful day at the Smithfield Street Bridge in Pittsburgh. The day he had lost his mother. The day he had found the strength to stand, even if it meant losing a piece of his soul in the process.

He hesitated at the mysterious figure's words. He paused to consider a different way, a way to make it right after so much death. Instead of a tug on the trigger, the shock of the recoil, rinse and repeat, there was the possibility of change.

Now Lincoln saw it for what it was: a dream. Standing before him was the reality of his situation. Marcus Engers, gun in hand, ready to shoot. Violence over discourse. Death over life.

It was the only way it could end. The only road left to Lincoln.

"It should have been you," Marcus said. His words were carried along the brisk wind of the winter night. North along the river, holiday lights beamed down highways and up buildings. The season provided hope for so many, while on the Red Bridge spanning the Des Moines River there was only darkness.

"It doesn't have to be this way," Lincoln replied. He kept his weapon low, the safety engaged. He fought against the current, struggling to chip away at the hate in the man's eyes. "We can fix this, Marcus."

The deformed sniper chuckled at the sentiment. "You're so far gone, yet you can't see it. You and your DSA. You're chasing something you can't even fathom."

"You're right. I can't. That's why I want to help. Please, Marcus, you have to let me help."

"You *are* helping me, pal," Marcus said. "The Witness is gone. I blew it. I'm a dead man no matter the outcome now. But to have the opportunity to take you with me? That's how it gets fixed. For me anyway."

"Don't, Marcus," Lincoln said. His sidearm shot up, the enhanced assassin unafraid in the face of the weapon. "Don't..."

They circled each other along the bridge. The cracking of ice sheets along the coast below accompanied their shifting steps as they took the measure of the other. Lincoln tensed, eyes begging his companion for a sign—a way out of the dark.

"The hell with this," Marcus muttered. His finger slammed against the trigger and a rush of air snapped the silence.

Lincoln dove to his side and fired. The chamber echoed, the bullet raging from the barrel to its target—center mass. Marcus' eyes widened for an instant before a smile grew on his face.

The green light tucked under his skin dimmed. Marcus' weapon skittered away from him, dropped from the impact. He spit blood across the pavement, before the massive weight of his body caused him to stagger back to the edge of the road. The railing was too close, the force of the blow too great to stop him from upending.

"No!" Lincoln bellowed. He fought for his feet, leaping for his dying friend. Lincoln snatched Marcus' hand as it slipped from the railing. He screamed at the pain in holding his massive frame. His gloves were slick and his grip tenuous to begin with. "Help... help me, Marcus. I'm not... I'm not strong enough."

Blood streamed along Marcus' lips and coated his teeth. "I know. That's why I win."

Marcus fell. His body shattered the thin shelf of ice along the river. He sank beneath the surface, his wide right eye never blinking, never looking away from the anguish on Lincoln's face.

He took that final revenge with him to the end.

Lincoln watched in horror as Marcus was lost to the water. When he no longer viewed any sign of Marcus in the darkness of the river, he collapsed along the railing. Hard sobs shook his exhausted body at the loss of another life—another one he took from the world. Nothing could shake that from him, nothing helped ease the pain of taking a life. Especially one saved, one cherished for so long.

Marcus' smile haunted Lincoln. It followed him as he managed to leave the cold comfort of the railing for the middle of the bridge. The pistol sat on the pavement as a further taunt, a reminder of how things could have gone the other way.

The clip dislodged, the contents mocking Lincoln's quick reflexes. It was filled with blanks. The entire confrontation had been a ruse to push Lincoln to act—to cause more pain in living than his death would bring. To Marcus, Lincoln had already taken everything. What else did Marcus have left besides his life, and Lincoln obliged without thought.

He was a killer, through and through, no matter how much he protested.

Lincoln threw the gun aside, letting it skid across the ice and into the waiting watery grave. The tired agent stood in the center of the bridge, eyes wavering on the choice before him.

To one side was the Savery and a situation of his own making. Two men were dead. Explanations were needed, no matter the consequences. Metcalf had to be notified and the DSA had to be offered a chance to clarify the truth behind what he had learned—if such a thing was possible at this point.

Then Lincoln recalled the message left by the Witness.

I promised you answers and delivered, Lincoln. You need me. More than you know.

The truth of the matter.

Sirens blared downtown, streaming from the Savery toward the river. Alarms rang out over the dead men and the man who had put them down. The past threatened to drown him as easily as it had Marcus.

Lincoln turned toward the far side of the Red Bridge. Beyond lay shadows, nothing but a growing darkness. The unknowable future he always feared.

The Witness held answers, and Lincoln needed them. He

needed to make the events of today right. To make sense of everything.

No matter what the future held.

CHAPTER TWENTY-EIGHT

The cap from the beer rattled along the floor. Ben took a long sip, savoring the bitter taste before swallowing hard. He retrieved the fleeing top and tossed it into the trash before heading into the living room.

Despite the boxes lining the closets and tucked in the corners of every room, Ben's apartment remained sparse. It had been two months since his arrival to Bethesda and he hadn't bothered to even fill the two-bedroom space, let alone unpack. Not that many family belongings had made the trek from Buffalo. A few photos decorated the mantel, treasured moments he was unwilling to relinquish.

What little furniture occupied the domicile came directly from the DSA. A couch and recliner rested in the living room. There was a bed in one room with matching dresser and nightstand. The desk set up in the spare room gave him a quiet place to work, not that he brought much home with him from the office.

Tonight was different. A single object sat centered on the oak tabletop. The Grissom File.

The case weighed on him. The knowledge of where it came from, of who had brought the fate of his predecessor before him, clouded the facts tucked within. Sullivan tested him on every level. From the retrieval spot ordered, to Ben's false assessment hearing, Sullivan challenged him. He monitored each reaction and pulled at Ben's core as a means of identifying key characteristics to decide his loyalty.

The file was the final measurement. If he found out the truth, Sullivan's coercion would be complete. Metcalf had sent the man, one deemed fit to head the DSA in her place, to his death. In doing so, she earned her fate — Metcalf had earned Ben's betrayal.

Was that what this was? A betrayal of a woman Ben barely knew? Metcalf had recruited him, saved him, and allowed him to continue to work — to find a new purpose in this world. But was it really his choice to make?

The surveillance Sullivan had managed to secure cast that in a new light. She had watched Ben for years, according to the images gleaned from the deputy director. She spent years tracking his career, monitoring his friends and their activities. She learned everything about him, long before Horace Waters and the frame job that had ruined his life.

Her surveillance of him continued to the present day. She tracked him before and after his shift — never giving him an inch of trust, always in control of his actions. How could he view Sullivan's offer as a betrayal when every step Metcalf took displayed the lack of faith in their relationship?

He took another sip, more bitter than the last, and he swallowed it down before setting the bottle on the desk. He loomed over the file, the contents still locked inside.

Sullivan's offer followed him. A return to Buffalo, a return to a life he missed. It was a chance to find Emily Wright, to remove the target placed on her thanks to his ignorance over his current assignment. Locating her brought with it the possibility of rekindling feelings they had never pursued while partners on the force. Sullivan was providing him with the chance to live his own life — to finally step out of his father's shadow and discover his own path.

Metcalf or Sullivan? The choice stood before him, and the question plagued him. No answer presented itself, and there was no clear direction out of the murky swamp threatening to drag him into the center of the power struggle.

No, the only way to find the answers was to learn the truth — about everything.

The wary agent pulled the chair away from the desk, then settled on the uncomfortable cushion. He rubbed his eyes, hand spread across the cover. Every question started with Jacob Grissom. From Ben's recruitment, to Sullivan's rise to deputy director, and Metcalf's secrecy — all began with a man Ben knew nothing about.

It was time to change that.

The file opened under his delicate fingers. He had to know the truth, not only about Grissom but about the DSA, once and for all.

CHAPTER TWENTY-NINE

A low groan escaped Zac's lips when he collapsed into his waiting chair. The dim light of the computer screen greeted him and his password brought the console to life.

Work had piled up, and he noticed the queue from the day awaiting approvals by him. Adler had done an admirable job. The flow had been maintained and cases were cleaned up or outright solved by the team. Metcalf would be pleased by her new recruit, which did little to settle Zac's nerves at her involvement in the first place. This was his domain, and the assignment of a stranger into his midst made the hair on the back of his neck stand on end.

He was grateful for the day he'd had away from it all. It had been a chance to do some good for one person he knew, instead of the strangers whose cases ran like a blur in a never-ending stream of work.

Morgan had needed him, and he had been there. What came of it was not his business; if it meant a small comfort for the woman, he considered the day a victory. Her story saddened him, the shadow of her past revealing Morgan in a new light. It was one he was grateful to view, even for an instant.

Zac clicked away from the flow of work. Cases could wait a few minutes more. A red light blinked along his extension, messages waiting to be heard. His wife, Claire, no doubt wondered when he would be home. He never called, never made an effort to pull her into his world. He had meant to inform her of the longer-than-usual day, the needs of a colleague taking precedence over his commitment to her and their son. Yet he had failed to call.

He picked up the phone, ignoring the message, and began to dial. When he reached the sixth digit he paused. The late hour on the clock stopped him and he hung up. Alex needed his rest. So did Claire. His schedule was not their own.

An excuse? Zac wasn't sure. Was there another reason he refused to make the call? Another reason he didn't want to hear his wife's voice? Zac pulled his cell from his pocket. He sent a quick text to satisfy his wife and his doubt.

He sucked in his gut and pulled his chair in close to the desk. Expert hands glided along the keyboard, attempting to rummage through the day's events. Instead of the workflow coming across his screen, a priority alert demanded his attention. Zac had set up dozens of them, most pertaining to the men and women of the DSA. It was how he'd learned so quickly about Tyrese Dunleavy and why he had been so rapid in his response to send Morgan to Mt. Sinai to be at her brother's side.

The alert related to a double homicide at a hotel. It wasn't their usual case profile, especially given how fresh the crime scene appeared, yet something pinged Zac's intricate system. He scanned through the files. The bodies had been found on the 11th floor of the Savery Hotel earlier that day.

Des Moines, Iowa. Why does that sound so familiar?

Zac plugged in a search through the Archive, the DSA's computerized records of hundreds of thousands of documents dating back decades. Only one item came back: the assassination of a prominent senator.

"Holy. This can't be—"

Do you know where Lincoln MacKenzie is currently?

The answer crystallized. Sullivan's fears over the whereabouts of their missing agent were justified by the evidence presented on the screen. Zac read the report again, details still filtering in through the various forensics and security brought in by the downtown Des Moines hotel.

Once everything pooled into view, Zac compiled a report. He attached the information to an email, Sullivan listed as the recipient. He included Metcalf beside the deputy, then paused.

Lincoln was in the field, working in some capacity. Someone had put him in play, even though he was pulled from active duty. Only one person had the ability to do such a thing. But why would Metcalf do it behind Zac's back?

Zac removed the director from the message and sent it immediately. The digital envelope soared to his sent box. Footsteps approached and he closed the report before returning to the missed queue from the day.

Morgan stood in the shadows.

"Hey," Zac called. He stood, his chair rolling to the back wall with a loud thud. After he had pulled it once more into position, he nervously chuckled and approached the looming figure. "How is everything? I wasn't—"

She pulled him close with a kiss. Deep and passionate, her lips spread along his. His shock over the situation settled and he joined the act. His body warmed at her touch.

When she broke the kiss, Zac hovered on his toes—almost weightless. "Wow. I mean… what was that for?"

Her hand grazed his cheek, a smile spread wide. "A thank you."

Turning, Morgan slipped from view without another word. Zac's fingers paused along his lips, grazing the memory locked in place. He held tight to that feeling for a long time.

"Wow."

CHAPTER THIRTY

The same report sat in front of her for over an hour. Not a thick file, and not an extensive summary of the daily events missed during her stay in Fort Meade. No, this one pertained to a requisition for some additional cups in the break room; a subject she knew about intimately over the course of her day.

Still, the words blurred despite her having cleaned the lenses of her glasses more than once. Her focus faded to larger concerns, bigger issues unseen until only the past few hours.

Metcalf started with the issues at hand. She audited Sullivan on a number of levels — taking a closer look at his reports, emails, and even his internet searches. Everything had been done while in the confines of the DSA and even at home through remote access granted by the department. His phone remained off-limits for the moment. For that, she'd require a warrant, and with the Council up her ass about every little choice made, she imagined this would fall under the less-than good category.

She found little. There was nothing overtly hostile toward her. Questions had been asked of analysts about certain cases; each one was worded with a slant toward skeptical on a command level. One was asked why certain personnel were specifically assigned to tasks. Another query from the deputy director sought out how approvals were finalized on an open case from a sister agency. They appeared to be inquiries into the DSA's internal process, and had she made the observation a week ago she would have thought as much.

Now she knew it for what it was: fishing for information to use against her.

It was all her own fault. The DSA was her weapon of choice,

one proudly used in her pursuit of justice. Instead of embracing those around her, she had pawned off the task to her subordinates. Grissom had filled that role, one she had never been comfortable with or deemed important enough. Metcalf had allowed the dismal morale to take root and Sullivan plucked the ripe weed for his own agenda.

Her team had floundered thanks to her mistake. Ben refused to answer her calls. She was not surprised, considering the number of secrets kept from him. He needed someone to trust, someone to turn to as his entire world slipped from him, and instead of assisting him she had sent Zac to spy on him.

Morgan was missing, her sudden departure throwing up more red flags, yet Metcalf was unable to ascertain the details from those she questioned upon returning to the warehouse. One day, however, was not cause for major concern considering Lincoln's absence. Days had gone by without an update; his last message to Stephanie was nothing short of a cry for help unanswered by anyone at the DSA.

A short knock at the door ended her ruminations. Her glasses fell on top of the unimportant report as Zac entered.

"I didn't think you were here today," she muttered.

"I am," Zac answered. He held his tablet at his side and carried a pensive look on his face.

"Right," she said, unsure of the sharpness of his tone. "Getting difficult to keep track, I guess."

His brow furrowed and she waved him off.

"Never mind," she said. "What is it?"

The tablet was extended and she took it in hand. Zac pointed to the headline at the bottom of the screen. "Two dead in Des Moines. Still a local matter, but our system flagged it."

"Des Moines?"

"It happened at a hotel downtown." He waited for her to jump into the conversation. She remained silent, letting him lead the exchange to its conclusion despite knowing where the road ended. "The Savery."

"No," she whispered. She read through the article rapidly. There were only preliminaries so far, nothing too damning from what she noted. She passed the small device back and Zac swiped along to another item.

"It gets worse."

"How much worse?"

"The victims were being kept under wraps. No disclosure of their identities, not even internally."

"They were government agents?"

He tapped the screen. "Army Intelligence. Working under General Adams."

"What?" she exclaimed. She stood, hands poised at the edge of her desk. "Any idea what they were doing there?"

"Not a clue."

"Okay…"

Zac huffed. "You're really going to play this game with me?"

"I'm not playing at anything, Zac," Metcalf replied, her words just as cold as her gaze. His insubordination had grown since Chicago, his anger over her leadership bordering on requiring disciplinary action. "What aren't you telling me?"

"I was about to ask the same thing."

"This is fun, Zac, but I assure you—"

He dropped the tablet on the desk. "What was the operation in Des Moines, Susan?"

The image blurred on the tablet and she reached for it slowly. "I don't understand."

"Of course you do," Zac snapped. "This is you through and through. Keeping secrets. Working around the systems we have in place, all for your own agenda."

"Zac, that isn't—"

He pointed to the screen. An image of their missing field agent filled the screen. In the photo, he fled from the hotel right before the two men were found dead.

"Why was Lincoln in that room?" Zac asked. "Why did he kill those men?"

"Lincoln."

"Hotel security picked this up on their internal feed."

Metcalf flipped through, recognizing Lincoln's Jeep found in the attached parking garage—now evidence for the investigation. How much did they know? How much did they have? What *was* Lincoln doing there, and why had he failed to share his situation with Stephanie?

"Who else?" she asked, the strength in her voice ebbing. "Who else has this information?"

Zac hesitated, tucking the tablet under his arm. His gaze was locked on the desk, never on her. "No one."

A lie, and she caught him in it. A test she hated to give. Her audit of Sullivan's emails had brought a new item to the list before she had finished. She had yet to open the item, believing the message to be unimportant to her search, but the subject clearly mentioned Lincoln and Des Moines. Zac had lied to cover his tie to Sullivan.

What else was he lying about? What else was he telling Sullivan behind her back?

"Zac?"

"The locals are working the case so far," Zac said, clearing his throat. "Should I put in a request to assist?"

The correct answer was yes. It was the one his eyes screamed at her to give. That road led to Lincoln's arrest and the divulging of the operation assigned to him. The Witness. The spectacled figure was still in the wind, as was the man after him. She needed Zac out of it completely.

"No," she said. "I'll take it from here."

"That's not—"

"I'm aware of procedure, Zac," Metcalf confirmed. "I'll handle it."

"Right." He backed away for the door, his disgust palpable. There was no choice in the matter, not now. With him sharing information with Sullivan, the best option was to keep him in the dark, though every instinct bellowed for her to trust Zac and to make amends.

He stopped at the door, pivoting back to her. "What was he doing there, Susan? What the *hell* was he doing there?"

Metcalf sat calmly, hands tucked neat in her lap. "I'll be sure to ask him."

The door slammed shut behind Zac, the answer not to his liking. It was all she had to offer. A truth, in a way. The only one left to her.

She was as lost as any of them. Two men were dead in Des Moines, and there was no utterance of the Witness in the initial report. What had happened in that room?

"What did he tell you, Lincoln?"

And what am I going to do with you now?

ABOUT THE AUTHOR

Lou Paduano is the author of the Greystone series of urban fantasy adventures, which follow Detective Greg Loren and Soriya Greystone as they hunt myths, monsters, and legends in the city of Portents.

He is also the author of the conspiracy thriller series, The DSA, a serialized tale about a clandestine government agency trying to discover the true power behind humanity's future.

He lives in Grand Island, New York with his wife and three daughters. Sign up for his e-mail list for free content as well as updates on future releases at loupaduano.com.

THE GREYSTONE SAGA

AVAILABLE NOW

Follow the adventures of Soriya Greystone and Detective Greg Loren as they hunt dangerous myths and legends in the city of Portents.

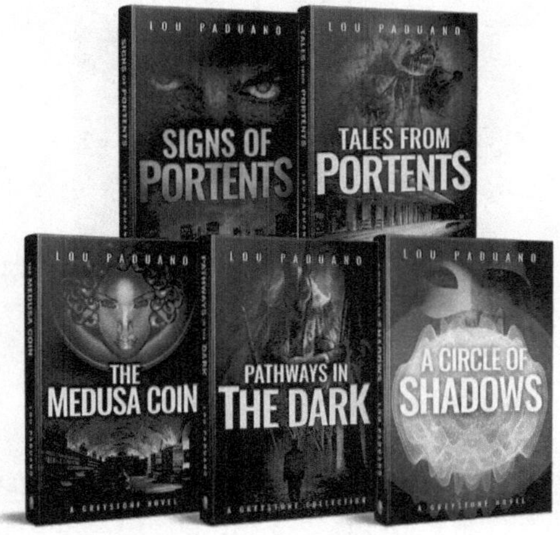

BOOK ONE - SIGNS OF PORTENTS
BOOK TWO - TALES FROM PORTENTS
BOOK THREE - THE MEDUSA COIN
BOOK FOUR - PATHWAYS IN THE DARK
BOOK FIVE - A CIRCLE OF SHADOWS

ALSO AVAILABLE NOW

It's her first case and it might be her last.

Soriya has worked her entire life to become the Greystone — protector of her city, Portents, against the growing shadows of myth and legend. All her efforts are in jeopardy when she is struck down by the destructive power of the Minotaur.

Soriya must now find a new path. Only one thing is certain — she's going to need help.

The secrets of Soriya's training are revealed in the first adventure of this new Greystone trilogy.

THE DSA CONTINUES IN…

Abigail Winslow, the DSA's latest recruit, is dead.

Unsure of who to trust anymore after learning the truth behind Agent Jacob Grissom's death, Ben Riley attempts to track down Winslow's killer without the use of the agency's resources. Facing a locked room murder, Ben turns to his only suspect for assistance—Cal Cooper, an attorney with a secret.

He sees ghosts—everywhere.

Thrust into a world he refuses to believe in, Ben must evade the danger posed by those beyond the veil and put his faith in a stranger to discover the murderer in their midst.

Unfortunately, Ben's line of inquiry may have made him the next target.